GAME MASTER

Game On

David Clark

CONTENTS

1

Robert had no idea how long he and his friends have been trapped in a box barely big enough to stand up in; much less to stretch out in. It was dark and the air was hot and stale, even with the holes in the wall and the slits in the floor. A sense of depression and despair hung heavy over the group. It had been a while since any of the others had said anything. They yelled for what seemed like hours, but it was closer to just minutes. After no response from outside, each person pulled within themselves to ponder their situation in their own little space of their cramped confines.

For the first few minutes, the six friends thought this was just an accident. They hoped Christopher was stuck in the elevator, and can't get out to let them through. As time wore on, that dissipated into nothing. Along with any hope they would be let out soon.

When Michelle turned on her cellphone, they gained their first real look at their situation. With each detail they observed, any lingering hope that this was all a mistake, or even a joke, disintegrated. There was one truth that was now clear for them all to see. Their friend of the last several weeks led them here intending to trap them and, well, they don't know what else yet. In fact, no one speculated about it out loud, but they were thinking about it; it consumed Robert.

In this dark solitude all he could do was think. His mind raced through the possibilities; from ransom to murder and the more demented. He thought back to every interaction with Christopher over the last several weeks for anything that might give him a clue, a direction, a hint at what his motive might be. No matter how many times he reviewed it, nothing stood out. What was yet to come was anyone's guess.

As he searched for answers, Robert was quick to discount the thought of ransom, he had no money, neither did Amy or his family. Then the thought, maybe someone else was the target emerged. He knew little about each of them; only what they told him or disclosed in other ways. It was possible that any one of them was hiding a secret life, something rather common with people you meet online (like he did each of these friends). Some even created a new persona. Are they who each claim to be or is this a fake life they concocted for the online world?

Could anyone, or several, of them have something in their past that made them a target? Something someone would want to get revenge for or to hold for ransom?

There was no way Robert could know. A part of him that wanted to ask, but how do you ask a question like that? "Hey, guys, has anyone here done anything that might cause someone to want to kidnap you?"

They could be the target and not even know it. Just asking that question might single one person out and the rest would attack or isolate them. That would be the worst case. To survive, Robert knew they must work together as a team.

There was that sound again: a machine of some sort starting up. When it started, you could hear it muffled in the distance and feel a strong vibration throughout the box. Other than the rustling of someone in the box trying to get comfortable, it was the only sound Robert had heard for the past few hours.

Sitting there in the darkness, he reviewed the images of the box stored in his mind. He turned each image around and around, looking for a weakness, a way out. There were no exposed joints, screw or nail holes. The door they came through had no exposed hinges or doorknobs on their side. No perceived weak spots at all. Each pass over the details resulted in the same conclusion. There was no way to escape, at least not until Christopher made his next move.

With that futile analysis completed, again, his mind shifted back to the question of why. What good would it do to just trap a group of people in a box and leave them? There was a bigger plan than just holding them in this box. There must be, or was there?

Over and over the questions cycled through Robert, with no answers to be found. The mental gymnastics were tiring. One fact was for sure, this was not something he believed could happen in his wildest dreams when he first met this great group of friends. Back then, it was all about fun and games.

2

"Gotcha, Biotch!", a voice exclaimed while one fist pumped in the air and the other maintained a firm grip on the game controller.

An adolescent voice protested the celebrated conquest through the headset, "That wasn't fair! I wasn't ready."

Back engaged in a battle that took place in a non-existing universe of ones and zeros, broadcast across sixteen other monitors around the world, various bodiless conversations took place via headsets worn by participants who have taken on personas like Killazilla, EyeShotUREye, MadUBe, WhoMe, and BOB with no reference to who they were in the real world. These conversations were not earth-shattering deep conversations that would solve world hunger by any means. They were more of a casual nature.

EyeShotUREye taunted his most recent victim over the open mic, "Tell it to your mother. Oh, and tell her I will be over later to spank that ass!"

Another voice chimed in, "Come on guys. Keep it clean, there could be little kids in here."

ULose responded with a voice that sounded like a six-year-old boy: "No kids here."

The rest of the room threw in their two cents in fake high-pitched voices: "No kids here. Say hi to your mom for me."

While the intelligent verbal barrage took place, EyeShotUrEye hunted down the last participant in the game, winning the Last Man Standing match. The players returned to the lobby and checked their match statistics, current rank, and any special perks they earned during the game. Once the stats were reviewed and bragged about, the wait for the next game ensued.

Some players left and said their goodbyes, while new players joined for the first time. The game was played all around the world making the concept of time irrelevant. It could be two in the afternoon for one player and two in the morning for others. Most had no sense of the actual time; they have been playing the same game for hours in total darkness. Pyramids of empty, colorful caffeinated energy drink cans and remnants of junk food decorated their room.

The passage of time paused while immersed in this world. Playing for days, only to stop to retrieve rudimentary microwaved nourishment that contributed to the global obesity problem, and an occasional bathroom break, was not unheard of. In fact, the world record for playing this kind of video game was one hundred and thirty-five hours straight. So, twelve, sixteen, or twenty hours was rather common, which made the question repeated at the end of every game somewhat rhetorical: "Do you want to play another?"

Killazilla confirmed the obvious, "Of course. Let's go. I'm going to win this time. Watch out!"

Killazilla was nineteen-year-old Robert Deluiz. He lived in a simple one-bedroom apartment in La Jolla California with his high school girlfriend, Amy Carter. It was 3:50 pm on a Friday afternoon in his world. His girlfriend was at work while he enjoyed the first day of a four-day weekend at the end of his second semester at San Diego Community College. With no homework, classes, or work until Tuesday, he wanted to unwind and enjoy the next four days. That included spending a significant amount of time online waging mindless war in the digital universe. He knew he needed to log off when Amy came home; she was not a fan of what she called a "waste of time." So, he tried to limit his game time when she was home to while she was on her laptop doing homework or reading the news, but when she was away, it was game on!

While waiting for the new game to start, an envelope appeared at the top of the screen. The preview showed it was a game invite from someone named UDiedPlaying. Robert ignored it and the game started. Eleven of the sixteen players remained from the last game; five players were new. Once the match opened, he announced, "Fresh meat for my mad skills!"

The round did not equal Robert's expectations; he was the second person killed and relinquished to sitting and watching for twenty minutes as others played out the game. As entertaining as it was to watch others play, and take part in the taunting, it didn't match playing yourself.

Back in the lobby, he didn't bother to check his statistics due to his lackluster performance; nothing should have changed. The cycle of game life continued, some left and others joined. One of the new members was the same person who sent him the game invite earlier, UDiedPlaying. They probably gave up waiting for him to accept the invitation and used a game option that let you join the same lobby as another player. No problems with that; the more the merrier.

Round after round, the cycle of players leaving and joining continued for the rest of the afternoon. UDiedPlaying left a few rounds ago and sent Robert another private game invite. Robert considered it for a second. They were good, why not?

He accepted and joined. There were already five players in the lobby, and compared to the other lobbies he had been in that day, they were quiet. Two more joined to bring the total to eight players and the game set them up into two random teams of four. Robert, Killazilla, was on the same team with UDiedPlaying. In a matter of minutes, the team hunted down everyone on the other team. Everyone but one. For the first time since the game started, a few broke their silence and cracked jokes, including UDiedPlaying. He sounded like an older man, but that didn't stop him from making childish jokes at the expense of the remaining opponent. All four members of their team talked and worked together to locate and trap the last target.

TPBungHole called them out, "Come on out. We have some nice bullets for you." The whole team laughed at that. It was too bad the other team couldn't hear their comments.

Killazilla took a quick look around the corner at where he thought the last player was. A quick, and errant, return shot confirmed the position. The four players worked together and coordinated the attack to ensure someone took them down, even if that meant running into a trap and losing a few of their own team.

Once everyone was set up, UDiedPlaying gave the order, "GO!"

With that command, four members came around the building and unloaded on IZtheBest. The graphic showed Killazilla made the final shot.

Once back in the lobby, Robert announced he needed to call it a day, his girlfriend should be home soon. The occupants in the room begged him to stay. UDiedPlaying made a passionate plea, but Robert had to go. He logged out and turned off the game.

Robert put the controller back with the console and turned the television back to a random cable channel as the lock on the door clicked. He greeted Amy, "Hey baby, how was work?"

"It was a long... long day, but I can't wait to get out of here and celebrate. Are you ready?"

Robert stood up off the sofa he had been planted in for the last several hours and replied, "Just finished getting ready. Let's go!"

3

It was the afternoon on day two of Robert's four-day weekend and Amy just left for her sister's baby shower, giving him three to four hours alone in the apartment. There was no need for him to wonder how he will spend that time, it was more than enough time to wage war in the digital universe. Amy would think spending several hours on a game was a childish waste of time, but to Robert it is both social and mentally stimulating like a complex puzzle. One where you run around shooting people and exhibit the social skills of any middle school locker room.

He grabbed the controller and switched on the console. Before he even launched the game, the counter of items in his inbox got his attention. Three hundred and eighty-three messages. He blinked to check if he saw that number clearly, he did; three hundred and eighty-three! More than a tad bit curious about all these messages, he checked his inbox. All of them, every single one of them, were game invites from UDiedPlaying. Robert muttered to himself, "Dang dude. What the hell?"

He thought about responding to him, to ask him to leave him alone or something, but ignored him and searched for an open lobby. With only a few hours to enjoy he had no time to waste on what was in his inbox.

Once logged in and in an existing lobby, notifications flashed for another seven invites. He bet he knew who those were from. Becoming annoyed, he ignored them again and prepared to play as the countdown to the start of the round was now at five seconds. The countdown hit zero, and the battle ensued in that digital world that felt all too real. With his feet up on the table (something he would never do if Amy was home) and leaning back in the couch, he zoned out engrossed in the world delivered to his eyes by the sixty-inch LCD display and to his ears through his headset. The world around him ceased to exist.

The round ended and the ritual changing of players commenced. Those either bored, tired, or looking for something different left and new players entered. Robert was engaged in an exchange with several other players that will never be compared to Macbeth or any other literary wonder and does not notice UDiedPlaying has entered the game lobby. The witty repartee continued with comments such as, "your talent stinks like my farts" and "do you want me to send pictures I took of your mother?"

The countdown in the lobby hit ten seconds and the game divided the sixteen players into two teams of eight. Only then did Robert notice who was on his team. He wondered to himself *why is this guy following him around.*

He muted that player to avoid hearing him during the game. When the game started, his team scattered around the virtual map. Some looked for that perfect sniper perch to gain an advantage over the others that want to run out in the open; others took the tact of duck and cover around the buildings while he searched for the tale-tell red flag above an opponent's head.

Muffled sounds of gunshots and explosions filled the background, signaling some had engaged each other. The kill notifications at the bottom of the screen reported several rapid deaths at the hands of UDiedPlaying. This game type allows players to rejoin the game after five seconds following their death. A popular type maximizing the opportunities for both those being killed and those doing the killing. His stalker's kill count racked up. Only two minutes into the twelve-minute game and he was up to eleven kills. Robert only had two. Combined with his performance last night, Robert was impressed and thought, "This guy isn't too bad."

He maneuvered around the cityscape they while looking for either a red or blue flag above each player's heads. Blue flags represented teammates and red flags were opponents; targets. They racked up more kills, UDiedPlaying led the way. Robert finally found an opposing player and pulled for a quick shot but was too late; another player on his team took his kill. He didn't have to even look at the message to see who. He knew.

The twelve-minute round ended and Robert's team won. It was not even close. The other team was very vocal in their disappointment, blaming one another. SpitinurEye was the target of all the suggestions on what he could do with himself, probably because he ended with twenty-nine deaths in total. Most of the players had double-digit deaths. While on the winning team, Robert was in complete shock. He had never seen a player rack up fifty or more kills before! He unmuted UDiedPlaying and offered his congratulations; it was well received.

Robert asked, "So what is your secret. I have never seen that many kills before?" He received the typical answer to that question in this setting, "Skills baby, all skills." Everyone laughed.

This continued for another thirty minutes with the results ending up the same. Whatever team UDiedPlaying was on, won. Robert found himself on the losing end of the random team assignment a few times. In one of those they killed him eighteen times. He noticed there were no missed shots; if he caught you in the open it was one shot and you are dead. You didn't have a chance to take a shot, as it seemed he was always prepared to shoot and knew the best places on the map that provided the best offensive spots while also staying protected.

The lobby broke up and Robert left in search of another game. While waiting for the system to match him with a lobby, he received a new invite that added to the large total already accumulated in his inbox. Having not found another lobby yet, he thought "what the heck, why not?" and accepted the invitation and joined the lobby. His abilities overcame his annoying persistence in Robert's head.

The lobby had nine other players inside already chatting it up when Robert joined. UDiedPlaying acknowledged his entrance and they debated what game-type and settings they should use. Some wanted a shorter game, five minutes, and others want a kill-marathon: twenty minutes of non-stop attack! They settled on the middle ground of ten minutes; the countdown began, and the players were divided up into random teams. Robert was not on UDiedPlaying's team, so this was going to be a long game for them.

Once inside you could only hear the members of your team, except for a quick five seconds when someone died allowing you to hear their pain.

MarieAntwerp was the first to speak, "So Killazilla, how many invites did he send you before you gave in and joined?"

Robert laughed before responding, "I lost count! I was ignoring them until he joined a lobby I was in and I saw how good he was." RobemBlind agreed with Robert: "Same here. That is pretty much why I accepted his invite too. I want to see all his tricks. He had seventy-three kills in a single game!"

Robert wondered if that number was right; that was more kills than most good teams get combined, not just a single player.

"Seventy-three? Are you serious?"

"Yep, seventy-three. I haven't seen him with less than forty kills in any game yet--I swear!"

MarieAntwerp concurred, "He killed me at least twenty times in the same game once. I thought he was cheating at first, but then I figured out he knew the maps better than I know my own room."

Robert wondered if he could learn something from this guy. He considered himself a good player, but this guy was on a different level. If he could pick up any tips, it would be great. Right now, though, his focus was avoiding his line of sight and becoming another victim as he racked up the kills.

MarieAntwerp started a casual conversation. "So KillaZilla, what side of San Diego are you in?"

"Just outside in La Jolla. How did you know?"

"We are all from the same area. Christopher looks at someone's profile before inviting anyone. This lobby is all local people."

Robert checked the list of players in the game. That was the first time Robert has heard what sounds like a real name online in months, but there was no one using that name in the game. So, he asked, "Christopher?"

"Oh sorry," MarieAntwerp replied. "UDiedPlaying is Christopher. He organized our group together. I am Mary."

"Hi, Mary, I am Robert."

RobemBlind interjected, "My name is Doug, and if you guys are done blabbing, can you see if you can locate where that bastard is. He has shot me four times in a row and I never saw him!"

BOB reported, "I have no idea where he is, I am not moving until someone finds him. And yes, I am Bob. I know, original name."

OICU ran to the other side of the road from Bob and provided intel to the team. "Hey Bob, he is close to us. I am over here across from you and I can hear his shots. I am Kevin, nice to meet you Robert."

"He is over here by the subway entrance. He shot me, but I saw him first." SkirtsnDirt reported. "Since we are doing introductions, I am Michelle, his latest victim."

Robert was close to the subway. He moved back against the wall and swiveled his control stick back and forth to look to either side to see if he can see where he is. It looked like he may have found a sniper perch and was camping there; that was a new tactic for him. Robert had played with Christopher a few times before and he never saw him camp in one spot before. Looking at both high and low spots, Robert thought he saw him sitting on top of a building overhang. The spot was partially protected by a large truck. He took aim and tried to find an open shot when he heard the crack of a gun going off through his headset; the game notified him of a detail he already knew. He was dead.

"I found him. He is up on the theatre sign across from the subway entrance. I don't think we can get a clean shot at him."

Michelle said she would try, but that was a short-lived attack as seconds later Robert heard a gunshot and he saw the report that UDiedPlaying killed SkirtsnDirt, again.

Robert taunted her, "I see that worked Michelle."

The ten-minute game clock expired, and the torture was complete. Robert's team lost, the outcome was never in question. Final tally: Christopher racked up fifty-four kills and Robert's entire team had nine. Everyone returned to the lobby after a few moments of admiring the horrible statistics from that poor effort.

Something Robert heard during the game has him curious: everyone was from the same area. He asked, "So, everyone here is from the San Diego area?"

Christopher said, "Yep, that is at least the location they have on their profiles. I thought it would be fun to play with locals."

"That is cool. I am in La Jolla, just outside. Anyone else from La Jolla?"

StrangerEyez had been rather quiet the whole time, but finally broke their silence. "I am. Or I might as well be. I am in Pacific Beach, by the Kate Session Park."

They were near Robert; just south of him.

"You guys are south from me. I live in a warehouse by the I-5 local bypass on the northern side of things."

Shocked, Robert asked, "Christopher, you live in a warehouse?"

"Yeah." He chuckled before continuing. "It is not what it sounds like. I guess I need to stop saying I live in a warehouse; everyone reacts oddly when hearing that. My father owned this warehouse as part of his business, but he no longer needed it so, he gave it to me. I renovated the whole thing. It looks like a typical rusty metal warehouse on the outside, but on the inside, complete luxury. I have a twelve-foot video wall for TV and games; a high-end bathroom; a bedroom you would find in a mansion, and more space in the back. Tons and tons of space. I used to have my own paintball and laser tag thing setup in here for some friends to come over and use, but I recently tore that all down to start a new project."

"Wait, you have your own laser tag setup? Inside where you live?" Doug sounded jealous with that inquiry.

"I did, but like I said, I'm starting something else in that area now. I have about ten thousand square feet of area to work in."

"Wow, Christopher, if I had something like that setup, I would never leave home!" Robert agreed with Doug on that point. If he had that setup, why would he ever want to go anywhere else. Hell, you can build your own amusement park inside that space. He would setup an indoor race track. Maybe save space for something Amy wanted, or maybe not. With that much space free you could build anything you want and do like what Christopher does and tear it down when you grow tired of it and build something else.

Robert had enough of the talking and only had an hour left before Amy would be home. He wanted a couple more shots at Christopher before he had to call it quits for the day. "Let's go again. This time Chris, I will get you at least once."

"NEVER!" He screamed as the screen went dark to start the round.

4

Over the next several weeks, Robert joined the local lobby to practice his craft during any free moments. Through the hours of playing he learned many things. He became a master of almost every map, learning every advantage he could gather from observing Christopher, but it did not stop there. He learned more about his new friends.

Michelle was a thirty-two-year-old single mother of two, who played the game while her kids were at school or their father's. She worked part time with her best friend from college as a wedding planner and was an avid obstacle course racer and cross-fitter. If she was not online playing during the day, then she was out running on the beach conditioning herself for the next race.

Doug was a retired Military Veteran of sixteen years from Kentucky. He passed the time by volunteering with the local Veterans Administration facility and taking his jeep off-roading. He moved to San Diego just over four years ago to be closer to his son who was stationed at the local Naval base. That was the excuse he told everyone, but when you heard him talk it was obvious, he really moved to be closer to his five-year-old grandson; his off-roading co-pilot.

The second youngest in the group was Mary, a nineteen-year-old psychology student. Her love of video games came from growing up as the only girl in a family of five brothers who played. If she wanted to do anything with her brothers, it had to be that.

Bob's story was similar, his interest in the game developed after playing against his two pre-teen sons who lived with their mom in Philadelphia. When not battling them online, he was a commercial electrician.

Jill's background of a schoolteacher was surprising; she was the 'foul' mouth of the group. Michelle once joked, "Of course she uses that language, she is trapped in a room all day long with thirty brats!"

Jill said the language came from her sorority days. Everyone was "bitch this" and "whore that". She joined as the peppy former high-school cheerleader and was the instant target for the other girls. During pledge week they gave her the name *Barbie doll* because of her blonde hair and less than one-hundred-pound petite stature. Once she became a sister, she had to develop a backbone and dish it back, when she did, they immediately accepted her.

Kevin was a twenty-seven-year-old out of work actor from Illinois. He spent five years in Los Angeles trying to get a part in anything from a commercial to a big spot in a movie. After more rejections than he could remember, he gave up and moved in with his roommate from college. It started out as only staying for a few weeks while he looked for work, but a year later, he was still looking.

It shocked the entire lobby when Christopher told them about his life. Some were even skeptical since it is common for someone to lie about who they are online, but after all this time most felt they knew him and gave him the benefit of the doubt. He was a thirty-seven-year-old single white male, who lived in a converted warehouse that his dad used to use as part of his business. After his ninth broken bone by the age of five, they diagnosed him with brittle bone disease. His condition was so severe he could not walk. Instead, he used a wheelchair to get around. Because of his condition, his parents isolated and protected him from anything that resembled a regular childhood. He was home schooled and not allowed outside to play with the other children in the neighborhood, out of a fear that something would happen. This caused severe depression and behavior issues during his teenage years. His parents wanted to get him help but were afraid the doctors would tell them it was their fault for raising him so isolated. So, instead of getting him help they provided him an activity that would exercise his mind and provide him a social outlet while also keeping him safe: video games. The age of the online multi-player game was just beginning, and they believed this interaction would fill in for what he needed.

Over the years Christopher had not only played every multi-player game released, he mastered them. Spending hours upon hours playing, with nothing else to do, he learned every cheat and nuance of them all. For a while they were a challenge for him, but over time he learned the pattern of the game developers and they became predictable; though he still played as he enjoyed the interaction.

When he turned twenty-one, he begged his parents to allow him to start his own life. Uncomfortable with him moving out into a more traditional setting, his father offered a warehouse he was about to have torn down. A work crew renovated it up to modern code. Then the best sub-contractor in the area created a living space that was beyond comfortable and border lined with excessive. The entire setup was created to meet his every need while also being completely tailored to his condition. Built into the structure was a huge room with the best surround sound setup money could buy: a twelve-foot video wall, and a dedicated T-3 internet connection; dedicated for his games.

A few people doubted all this, as it sounded too good to be true, but Christopher sent pictures the other day through social media of the entire setup including the laser tag room he had built in an open area. He said a few years ago he developed a real close group of friends that lived local. They talked about wanting to go play laser tag. Christopher knew he could never join them but thought he could set something up and bring them to him. He worked with the same contractor that built his living space and had a laser tag course built and then invited everyone over for his twenty-fifth birthday party. It was a great time. Christopher said it was as close to playing a video game in real life as he had ever experienced. After that, he had a crew tear it down to clear room for other types of games in the space. This time doing much of the design work himself.

Several members of the group asked him if he ever left this home. He said he always wanted to but was too scared to take that risk. Even hitting a bump in his wheelchair too hard or at the wrong angle could cause his hips or back to fracture. His father put in a soft, cork-based flooring to create a stable floor. The elevator he used to go back and forth between floors was specially designed to avoid any sudden movements. It took him a minute to go one floor. There were spring-cushioned bumpers on every edge to provide a buffer in case he rolled his chair into one. They also cushioned the walls with pillow-type coverings to protect against any accidental impacts. A cleaning crew came by three times a week to clean every inch and repair any exposed dangers. A nurse called or stopped by once a day to check on his wellbeing. Christopher said the nurse got on his nerves at times thought. She wants to talk when she stops by and that interrupted his games, but this was a concession he had to give his parents to be allowed to live alone. It always worried them that something would happen, and he might lay there for hours with no one around to help. Luckily for him, his last broken bone was two years ago. He reached for an item on the second shelf in the refrigerator; he must have bumped it with his chair when reaching and an orange from the shelf above rolled off. It struck his forearm, breaking both the radius and ulna bones while leaving a severe bruise on his arm and legs where the orange came to rest. He was able to call for help within minutes that time.

They had become a tight-knit group, now spending several minutes catching up and chatting before starting the first game. Even during game play, most of the chat was more casual about life with a few interruptions of the more tactical nature. Robert considered each of them a close friend, just as he would someone he met at work or school.

Now this close group was officially a clan, a recognized group that played together against others in the game. They were not just any clan. They were a formidable clan that most avoided, while others sought them out to test their abilities against. The lore of their conquests littered the social media boards. The game was becoming too easy for them. They invented ways to make it more challenging. Using types of weapons that are only single shots, knives only, grenades only; anything to add complexity to the game. Their combined skills matched against the over-aggressive and lack of skill of the average player that runs around looking for targets, which takes a good amount of challenge out of it. Occasionally they ran into someone of similar talent, and those games they cherished; but those were far and few between.

5

The SanSquad (that is what they called themselves) had been together for several weeks now. Whether or not they played the game daily, they were part of each other's daily lives. They celebrated birthdays and offered a shoulder to lean on when real life stresses got to them. Doug was even helping Michelle with her oldest child's math homework. Mary and Jill went shopping a few times and Doug took Kevin off-roading out in the desert; Kevin said he barely survived Doug's wild driving just getting to the desert. As a group, they discussed getting together, but scheduling or other problems interfered. Now they were talking about it again and Mary would not take no for an answer.

She had it all planned out and set a date two weeks in the future, more than enough time to allow everyone to make arrangements. They would meet in Mission Park, the midpoint between where everyone lived, which made it the most convenient. She tried to come up with every solution so Christopher could join them, but failed. He brushed it off with his dry humor, "Why would I want to meet players who suck as bad as you?" or "If I met you, I would feel bad when I shoot you during a game."

The day arrived. Robert showed up first, but Doug arrived a few minutes later in a raised-up four-by-four that screamed Doug. Ten minutes later Michelle and Mary walked up, they decided to carpool since they were coming from the same area. Then Bob and Kevin staggered in over the next 20 minutes. The only no-show was Jill. She messaged everyone earlier saying she didn't think she could make it, her grandmother had become ill and she needed to check on her. Michelle and Mary stopped by to pick her up, but they said she was not there. They understood. Jill's parents died when she was nine in a tragic accident and her grandmother had raised her since. When Jill graduated college, her grandmother started showing early signs of Alzheimer's Disease. For the first few months everything was fine, but it progressed faster than any other patient her doctor had seen. It was a heart-breaking decision for her when the care became more than Jill could handle while working too, and it forced her to put her in a nursing facility. The costs and guilt of the decision created a tremendous amount of stress for Jill. We all told her over and over she made the best decision for her grandmother, but she still felt guilty. So, hearing that her grandmother was sick, and Jill was there instead of here was not a surprise. It was what Jill needed to do.

Once together, there was no need for introductions, they had talked for weeks and thanks to the shared pictures and video chats, all recognized each other. They walked from the park to a nearby coffee house to enjoy coffee, the ocean air, and casual and entertaining conversation. The game that brought them together barely came up. Instead, they talked as friends about anything and everything. They shared pictures of kids and spouses, talked of trips they planned to go on, Doug talked about all the spots in the world he has been deployed to, and work. What each of them did for work was a major topic, which was common when adults got together. Robert was surprised at how different each person's personality was compared to what he thought based on their online interactions. Doug was uptight and intense in the game but a relaxed jokester full of one-liners in real life. Mary was a complete flirt who checked out every guy in the group and every guy in the coffee shop. Michelle was more reserved compared to the online persona that often yells, "Take that, and come back if you want more," after every kill. He was curious if the others made any similar realizations about him. He believed he was the same online as out in the real world; maybe they all felt the same; it was how people see you that was different.

They took several pictures together and posted them on social media. Almost immediately, Christopher liked each photo. Robert had no doubt he was playing the game and watching social media updates to see what the group was up to. So, Robert made a suggestion to the others and they all agreed. They grabbed their coffee and headed back to Mission Park. After a brief search, they found a free table and crowded on the same side. Michelle took out her phone and held it out in front of the group as far as her arm could reach.

A box popped up on the screen with Christopher smiling inside. In unison, they greeted him, "Hi, Christopher."

"Hey guys, how is it going?"

Michelle decided to be the spokesperson of the group, "We are doing good. We are in Mission Park enjoying the sun and some coffee. What have you been up to?"

"Been playing a little, looking for new victims"—cough-- "I mean opponents."

"Finding anyone more fun to kill than Michelle?" Doug took a personal shot with that question and Michelle smirked.

"Nah, no one will ever be as fun as her. I have never heard a game controller smashing into sheetrock before until that time I killed her."

"Hey, you two, that was a onetime thing, and I have mellowed out since then." Michelle said with a pout planted on her face. "Well we were thinking about you and wanted to call and tell you hi."

"Thanks guys, it is nice to be thought about. Have fun." With that Christopher closed things on his side.

The quick disconnect took several of the group by surprise, but he was a deliberate no-nonsense person. Robert realized he probably felt we called to say hi and once we did, that was the end of the conversation.

Doug said, "He must have some bad players on the hook and wants to get back at trying for one hundred kills in a game." The others smirked and laughed at the comment because they each know it was a good possibility with him.

They spent another twenty minutes together finishing their coffee and talking about all things in life before bidding each other goodbye and going their separate ways. They knew they would talk later via social media and all meet again soon in the digital world dominated by the SanSquad.

6

Several weeks passed since the day in the park and the games continued as usual with one exception. They saw Christopher online, but he ignored their invites. When he did join them, he was not the fixture he used to be or as talkative during the games. Instead, he became business-like and left the banter to the others in the lobby. On social media he was active, but not super responsive to messages from anyone in the group.

Wondering if there is something wrong, the group elected Michelle to talk to him and ask if everything is okay. Later that afternoon, Michelle reached out to Christopher to talk, and he did not reply. By the end of the night, with no reply from Christopher, she let the others know she had not heard back from him.

When Robert saw the message from Michelle, he jumped into the game for a minute to see if he was on and, as he expected, he was. He selected to join the same lobby, but was only in there for a second or two before someone removed him. He tried again but received a message the host blocked him. A fact he found somewhat odd. He did not know who the host was, it may be a closed game. Robert thought if Christopher had seen him though he would have asked the host to let him stay. Hell, maybe this group was better competition. He heard the shower water turn off and logged out of the game before Amy caught him.

The next day Robert checked in with Michelle again. She still had not received a reply from Christopher yet. She knew he saw the message; she could see that in the indicator next to it, but she had grown concerned that Christopher was ignoring them. Robert tried to reassure her and agreed to message him, but first he checked to see if Christopher is online. As he expected, Christopher was online in the game. Robert tried to join his lobby and was allowed in. He heard Christopher's voice through his headset, but before Robert could say "hi", someone kicked him out again. He attempted to get back in and was blocked! He looked up and down his friends list for any of the SanSquad and saw Doug on and joined his lobby.

Robert told Doug about Christopher in the other group and how he believed he was the one who kept kicking him out of the lobby. That prompted an uncharacteristic "fuck him" from Doug. Robert didn't believe Christopher had meant any ill by it but decided to move on. That happened in friendships in the real world and online. People come in and out of your life, some flashed through and are barely memorable, some made a significant impact before moving on, and others stuck around forever. You never know who was which type when you first met them.

Over the next hour, most of the SanSquad joined Doug's game, and they picked up where they left off beating all comers. Though not as convincingly as they did when Christopher was on their team. After several games, Robert received a private message from UDiedPlaying. He waited until the next match, his most dominating performance of the day (twenty-two kills!). before he checked the message.

Hey Robert,

Sorry about earlier. An old friend was running that game. He has a close group he plays with and invited me in. I will be back soon. Tell the group I said hi.

Robert relayed the message to the gang, but it was met with a mixed reaction. Some were happy and looking forward to him returning, but Mary and Doug were less accepting. Mary brought up all the attempts to contact him over the last few days and he couldn't just say, "Hi guys, I am playing with an old friend. Talk soon," or something to that affect. Robert realized she had a point but tried to calm everyone down.

A few matches later, Christopher finally joined the lobby. "Hi guys, did you miss me?"

Michelle greeted him with a faux disappointment, "Dang it! He is back. I won't be the best player in the group anymore."

"What? You guys let her beat you while I was gone. I thought I trained you all better than that."

Jill tried to correct the misconception set by Michelle. "Did you become gullible while you were away? She couldn't beat a spider with the world's biggest shoe!"

"Gee, thanks Jill, I am not that bad. I have beat you a few times."

You could almost hear Christopher smile through the game. "There is the group I missed. Let's get this on!"

The gang was back together, any questions of ill will had disappeared in just moments. In the game, things picked up where they left off. Those on the opposite team from Christopher were doing anything they could to avoid him. Christopher was a silent killing machine, taking people out one at a time, repeatedly with no reaction. If it wasn't for the conversations after the game, you wouldn't know that he took great pleasure in being the dominant force. He was our leader and mentor in the game, and we were his obedient students.

Robert thought about the list of tasks he needed to complete before Amy returned home from her girl's night out and decided he needed to call it a night. "I got to go guys. I need to clean the kitchen before Amy gets back. I made mess earlier cooking for myself."

"Wait!" Christopher yelled.

Robert delayed bringing up the menu and shutting down until he found out what Christopher wanted.

"I feel bad for not being around for a while. I want to make it up to everyone."

Michelle still acting as spokesperson for the group, said, "Aww, that is sweet, but unnecessary. We understand about your old friend."

"Michelle, I am serious. I want to make it up. Why don't you guys come over one day? You can all check out my place and we can play in the same room on my video wall. It will be great!"

Robert, remembering Christopher's physical and medical condition, was worried that would be a big imposition on him. "Christopher, it isn't necessary. We don't want to make you go through any special effort or anything. Like Michelle said, we understand. We have all been there before."

"It's no problem at all. We can order pizzas; there is plenty of room. What do you all think?"

Doug was first to respond, "Sure, I am in. I loved the pictures of your place and have been curious to see it in person."

"Great!"

Michelle jumped in too, "Count on me as well."

Jill and Mary both agreed they would come.

"What about the rest of you guys? Do you want to come?"

Robert thought about it for a moment and then agreed to come over, "Sure, just let me know when."

"Kevin and Bob, what about you guys?"

In unison, "Sure."

"Great. I will send out a time, date, and address. We'll have a great time. I can even show you the latest project I am building in the back."

Robert asked, "What are you building back there now?"

"It's a secret. You can all see it when you are here. You will love it."

Mary gushed over the idea of a surprise, "Oh I love surprises! They make me all giddy and warm inside."

Christopher replied with a full belly-laugh, "Then this is right up your alley."

Robert noticed the mess in the kitchen out of the corner of this eye and said. "Guys, I have to go. Let me know when and where and I will be there. Night all!"

With that he pulled up the menu and turned the game off, moving his attention to that mess in the kitchen. He wondered; how did one person make that big of a mess ? I would have a better chance of beating Christopher than I do at cleaning this kitchen to a shine, he thought. If only I had a grenade like I do in the game. He laughed, thinking about the explanation: "I'm sorry Amy, I don't know what happened. I was in here fixing something to eat and I dropped a grenade. On the plus side, we don't need to clean the kitchen.... there is no kitchen!" That would be a direct path to the single life.

7

Robert was late. Well, late was not the right word, he was extremely late. He was due at Christopher's over twenty minutes ago. The directions Christopher gave him confused his GPS. It told him to turn after he had already passed the road. With each passing minute, he heard his phone periodically chime. Presumably messages from his friends asking where the hell he was.

He finally rounded the corner and pulled into what used to be a parking in front of the warehouse. The rest of the gang was outside directing him into a spot. Robert knew he needed to prepare himself for the ribbing of a lifetime.

"Hey Robert, we were about to send out a search party for you."

"Yeah--yeah, Doug. The GPS had me turning into a few buildings and off a few overpasses."

"Oh sure, blame the technology. You said the other day it was a direct shot up the I-5 for you." Michelle reminded him.

"So why are you guys still standing out here? Why didn't you go in?"

"Just waiting on the last of our team. Let's go in." With that, the seven of them approached the door. They paused for a second, looking back and forth at one another. Kevin flinched. "Oh, all right, Jesus. I will press the doorbell." Kevin reached out and pressed the doorbell. They didn't hear anything and wondered if it worked.

He was about to press it a second time when Christopher's voice blasted from an overhead speaker. "Hey guys. I was wondering when you would come in. I saw you all standing around on the security cams I have covering the entire property. Come on in." The door in front of them clicked and released open like it was spring loaded.

Feeling embarrassed, they single-filed in through the door and were taken aback by what their eyes saw. The pictures did not do Christopher's converted warehouse justice. The foyer was amazing by itself. The hardwood floor had a glossy finish so deep you can see your own reflection. The walls were covered sections of corrugated metal panels framed in reclaimed wood, creating an industrial feel. The lack of a ceiling and exposed rafters and polished stainless steel air conditioning ducts created an open feeling. Pendant-style lights hung from the rafters down to ten feet off the floor. To the left there was an odd square structure framed in I-beams and covered in a chain-link fence. It took only a few moments before an elevator car came into view, descending the structure, carrying Christopher and his wheelchair.

"Hey guys, welcome to my home." The elevator car settled on the floor and the doors opened automatically. Christopher rolled out. His appearance surprised Robert. He expected Christopher to look frailer because of his condition; other than the wheelchair he was the picture of health.

"Wow, Christopher! This is some place." Michelle looked around in awe.

"Thanks, but this is just the front door. Take the stairs and meet me up there for the real show." They headed for the stairs while Christopher rode back to the second floor.

As they climbed the floating stairs encased in a glass wall, the colossal size of where Christopher lived became clear. The stairs opened into a modern kitchen. Everything, not only the appliances, were stainless steel. The walls, cabinets, and countertops were all simple brushed stainless steel surfaces with rounded corners. There was not a square corner in the place. A bumper lined the bottom of the cabinets, just like Christopher said. The floor was some kind synthetic high gloss material that felt soft under their feet. Another detail that matched how Christopher described it.

The entire floor plan was open and clean. None of the rooms had ceilings. Like the foyer, they were open to the rafters of the warehouse. To the right was his living room or, better described as, his game room. Racks upon racks of servers and other machines created a noticeable hum. There was a custom-built console in the center of the room, also in the industrial style, that contained every game console known to exist and a projector that displayed the games up on a twelve-foot-wide screen on the wall only ten feet away.

"So, guys, now that you have seen the meat of it, what do you think?", Christopher asked while rolling off the elevator.

Robert said with wide-eyes, "This is awesome! I love the look and the openness. I have never seen an all-stainless kitchen; I like it. What is the floor?"

"The floor is cork with a synthetic polymer surface that reacts to points of force and provides a cushion to soften the impact. They use it on high-end indoor tracks and basketball courts. Hard enough to bounce a ball on, but reactive enough to minimize injury."

As he said that, Christopher threw his cell phone down on the floor catching everyone by surprise. "Oh, don't worry. It is not broken. Kevin, can you pick that up for me?"

Kevin picked it up and handed it to Christopher, who held it up to show that not only was it not cracked, but it still worked.

"My father's work crew colored and textured it to look like various surfaces. That hardwood you saw downstairs is this same substance. The tile floor you see in the living room over there, which also extends into my bedroom and bathroom, is the same substance. Just colored and textured to resemble another type of floor. The best part about them is the sound absorption. Without them this place would be an echo chamber, but I can watch TV or play a game using the surround-sound and hear a full rich sound."

Robert was impressed and slightly jealous; he would love to live in a place like this. He couldn't imagine many who wouldn't. Everywhere he looked was another area that grabbed his attention.

"Christopher, how much of the actual warehouse do you use? It looked huge from the outside and I didn't expect a two-story living setup."

"About a quarter. I have a small garage behind the living area and the rest of the space is for me to do with what I want."

Michelle refocused her attention from exploring the space, back to the conversation with the group, "Oh, your project space. You were going to show us what you are working on."

"Of course. I will give you all an up-close look at it later, but now help yourselves to some pizza on the island in the kitchen. There are all different drinks in the refrigerator and let's have fun!" With that, Christopher pressed the on button on the custom center-console and screen divided into eight boxes was projected on to the wall. The game login screen was displayed in each box. Robert checked to make sure his mouth was not hanging open; if he wasn't jealous before, he was now. This will be a fun afternoon.

8

Now this was how you play as a team, everyone in the same room and able to communicate both verbally and non-verbally. Robert worked closely with a few over the course of the afternoon to set up attacks resulting in ruckus cheers, high-fives, and their version of a touchdown dance. In one round, Kevin took out every member of the opposing team by himself. To celebrate, he ran a complete lap around the room screaming and spiked the controller into the soft cushion of the recliner he was sitting in.

Their opponents had no idea they were playing a team that sat together in the same room. It took Robert a few games to get used to all the information in front of him. A few times he found himself looking at someone else's screen and paid the ultimate price for his lack of attention in the game. Eventually he realized how to use it to his advance and glanced at the other screens to get a wider view of the around him. This actually saved him once, he was in the prone position working from a sniper spot and happened catch the sight of someone coming into the building he was in on Jill's screen.

The others seemed quite used to this setup. They worked together calling out targets to each other with a natural ease. Supposedly this is everyone's first time visiting Christopher, but they seem too comfortable; like they had done this before.

During one of the intermissions between games, Robert threw the question out to the group. "All right, what gives? You guys have all been here before, right?"

The entire group looked at him with a stunned look on their faces, but only Mary addressed the question. "Robert, what do you mean?"

"Watching you guys play. You are all so comfortable working together with multiple screens. I get lost and confused."

"You are an only child, aren't you?"

Robert didn't understand Bob's question, but answered anyway. "Yes, why?"

"You get used to doing this on a small scale if you play with or against someone on the same monitor, the game splits the screen in half. I have watched my boys play like that at times. Usually one of them accusing the other of cheating if they look at the other screen."

"Splits it in half? That would be too distracting to me." Robert had never played this with or against anyone before in the same room and definitely not on the same screen.

Doug shook his head in agreement with Robert as he stood up to stretch. "It is weird at first, but you soon learn to use it as an advantage. I have a few other friends that I get together with to play games. Everyone brings their own game unit and monitor. We all sit in the same room and work together like this. It is some of the best fun I have ever had."

"So that is how you do it, Doug. I was wondering why you were calling out threats and opportunities like it was nothing, and every time I look at all the screens, I get confused."

Mary assured Robert he would get used to it.

They dominated every match that afternoon. Game after game with the same result in a non-stop pace, only pausing every so often for someone to retrieve a piece of pizza or something to drink. Christopher disappeared for minutes at a time off-and-on throughout the afternoon, but always returned before the next game started. Most hardly notice, but Jill commented on it several times to different members of the group and eventually asked, "Christopher, is everything okay, I notice you keep leaving. Are we keeping you from anything?"

"Oh no, not at all. I was preparing to show you all something I'm working on later, so just checking to make sure everything's ready."

Michelle got up, "Is it ready? I have been dying to see it since you told us about it."

Christopher motioned with his hands for her to sit back down. "There is plenty of time for that. It's almost ready. It's hot back there so trying to get it to cool down before we go in. Let's play more. It'll be ready soon."

Another two hours and thousands of dead opponents later, Christopher left the lobby of the game and suggested a new activity. "All right, it should be cool enough now, how would you all like to take a break and see my project?"

Michelle, who had been eager to see it since they arrived was the first to agree, "Absolutely, it is about damn time, let's go."

"Alright, follow me." Christopher rolled his wheelchair through a door to his bedroom, which was as fantastic and industrial décor-inspired as the rest of the rooms. There was no ceiling to the room, like the others, but the back wall of this room did go all the way up to the rafters of the warehouse, creating a separation. This made sense to Robert. It would be impossible to heat or cool the entire warehouse and, if he did have cars in the attached garage, you don't want any fumes in the living space.

"Okay, it is right through this door." Christopher pointed to a door in the back of his bedroom. "You go on through. There's another door that'll lead to some stairs; just stop at the door. I need to go down the elevator. When I get down there, I will turn on the lights and tell you when to open the door and come down the stairs. See you in a few minutes."

Christopher wheeled out of the bedroom and back through his living area. Kevin opened the door and motioned everyone toward the opening. He bowed and with the worst English accent ever attempted he said, "After you, your majesties."

One at a time they walked through the door and into the darkness. Mary went first and Kevin pulled up the rear. He closed the door behind them sending the group into complete darkness.

"Kevin why did you close the door? It is completely dark now."

Doug chided, "Jill, are you scared of the dark?"

"Yes, and a little claustrophobic."

"Now you tell us. Kevin, can you open the door until Christopher gets everything setup for us?"

"Robert, I wish I could, but it's locked. The doorknob doesn't even turn."

Jill grunted and asked, "Mary can you move up a little?"

"No, I'm up as far as I can go at this end. I hope Christopher hurries. I'm starting to feel a little uncomfortable too."

A very loud groan echoed through the darkness.

Bob tried to loosen up the tension by imitating a vampire's voice, "Aww, the girls are scared of the dark." He failed. The only reaction was several deep sighs of disapproval from the trapped and increasingly uncomfortable group.

Seconds became minutes as the temperature rose in the room.

"Guys?"

Mary responded, "What?"

"You don't think this is a big joke Christopher is playing on us? We aren't just stuck in a closet for his amusement, are we?"

Bob replied, "Some joke."

Robert thought for a second; it was possible, but why?

Another couple of minutes passed, they were hot and completely over this. Jill struggled to stand still and Mary turned around and around, taking deep breaths trying to relax. No one had said much for the last few minutes, but the groans and sighs coming from all of them signaled everyone was beyond tired of this. The enthusiasm they once all shared was gone.

Doug was the first to break the silence. He banged on the wall calling out to Christopher, "Come on, Christopher, enough is enough! Open either door and let us out." But there was no response from outside. "Kevin, is there any way you can force the door open?"

"Let me try." Robert heard the solid sounding thuds of Kevin's shoulder ramming the door. "Doug, it is solid. It won't move at all. Mary is there any give in your door?"

Mary did not respond.

"Mary?"

Still nothing.

"Kevin, I think she's freaking out. Let me try to change places with her and I'll check the door."

Robert heard movement in front of him and felt people bumping into him as Doug squeezed around Mary. A few people let out a "Hey", followed by a "Sorry" from Doug as he pushed the first four people into one another as he moved.

"Alright, the doorknob is solid and locked. Let me try to put my shoulder into it." There was a big impact, then another, and another. Robert could feel the thuds reverberate through the floor as Doug put all he had into each shot. After several attempts the door stood firm.

"It's solid, but I think I hear something on the other side. I hear something that sounds like machinery. Christopher must be in there. Everyone yells, let's get his attention."

They banged on the walls and yelled; making a huge racket. Robert again felt the vibration through the floor. Where they suspended in the air? He joined in and jumped up and down to create even more noise. It produced a large vibration felt through the entire room. They continued this for what seemed like an hour but in reality, it was only a couple of minutes.

"Everyone stop, so I can listen at the door again."

Robert pushed his ear up against the wall as well to see if he can hear anything. There it was, the sound of machinery like Doug said. "I still hear it. Start again."

"Wait, I've had enough of this. Not sure why I didn't think about this before." Suddenly a light illuminated the space. Michelle had her cell phone out with the light on. "Is everyone okay?"

Mary broke her silence, "I am better now, thanks Michelle."

"I'm done with this game. I'm calling for help. Maybe Christopher was trapped in the elevator or something." The light dimmed as she and tones of her dialing 9-1-1 echoed in the room.

"Fuck! I have no signal. Does anyone else have their phone?"

Robert felt stupid, his was in his pocket. "I do, let me try." He turned his on to check and like Michelle's. "No signal either."

The rest of the group left their phones out where they were sitting. The mood in the tight room went from aggravated to hopeless. Michelle kept her phone on to provide some light. For the first time, Robert saw the cramp quarters they were trapped in. It was a simple plywood box. The floor, walls, and ceiling were all a type of plywood normally called OSB: Oriented Strand Board.

He looked to the front and was startled by what he saw, "Um, guys? Look at the door to the front? It's not a door."

What they thought was a door was only a piece of plywood with a doorknob attached. Doug slammed his fist into it as hard as he could; producing a thunderous sound that was only over-powered by him yelling: "WHAT THE FUCK!"

Robert continued his detailed survey of their surroundings. He looked for any nail or screw holes indicating where the studs were, thinking he might be able to kick through in between them, but instead of screw and nail holes he noticed the walls had rows of holes about a quarter inch wide. They occurred every four to six inches for the entire length of both walls. The ceiling was a solid piece of plywood with no seams, nails, or screws. These must be custom-built pieces of wood. Robert knew from working on his uncle's construction crew a few summers ago, that OSB came in four feet by eight-foot lengths. There should be at least one seam in the walls and ceiling.

He looked down for any kind of break or seam in the floor, but noticed something even more shocking. Someone cut a series of large slits in the wood. They were twelve to eighteen inches in length.

"Everyone move to one side or the other. I want to see the floor." The group shuffled, clearing the center of the floor and taking notice of what Robert saw.

"Robert, what the hell are those?"

"No clue Kevin, I have no clue."

The slits lined the entire floor from front to back, alternating in rows of four or five slits across with maybe six inches in between each row. "Look at the walls too, there are rows of holes drilled into them. It looks like hundreds of holes."

Michelle used her light to look through one of the holes in the wall. "Are they air holes? It has to still be dark outside or we would have seen a light coming in through all the holes in this thing."

These discoveries led Robert to a confusing conclusion: this was deliberate. All of it. They were lured here to be trapped in this box. Everything that happened over the last few months, he wondered, was it all a setup and why? There was time to think about that later, now they need to get out before they find out what was planned for them, because whatever it was, it would not be good.

"Does anyone see a seam or any screws or nails? I have been looking, but I don't see anything." Robert saw Doug's head looking around at the floor and walls.

"No, nothing. I've been looking for that. I work in construction and use this type of board all the time. I'm in shock there are no seams. These boards are normally no longer than eight feet."

Robert agreed, "I know. I've built a few things with my uncle and was thinking the same thing. If we can find a seam on a wall or floor, I have my pocketknife. I can try to cut the corner a little and then we should be able to kick it through."

"Can you try cutting through those?" Michelle says, pointing at the rows of cuts in the floor.

"If I can't find anything else, I'll try, but I don't think I can. This type of wood is almost impossible to cut through without a rip saw. Does anyone see anything else?"

Heads moved about looking at the floor and walls. Everyone then looked at Robert and shook their heads. There was only one option left and Robert knew it had next to no chance of success. He pulled out his pocketknife and flipped out the blade while crouching to the floor. He looked at the slits in front of him wondering if it mattered which one he chose; they all looked the same.

He picked the one closest to him. If he can cut a line connecting two of them, they should be able to kick and stomp on that area enough to make it break the rest of the way through. That should give them a good-sized hole to get out. Tilting the blade slightly to force the contact with the top edge of the slit, he ran the blade up and down at a furious pace, applying light pressure against the floor. He tried to cut as fast as he could. His arm and shoulder started to burn but he did not stop; he was on a mission. He forged on for the next few minutes until his forearm and hand gave up the ghost and could no longer hang on to the knife anymore. The knife fell from his hand, but the muscle cramps and spasms wouldn't allow his hand to open. Using his other hand, he tried to massage the pain out of it. After a few seconds the pain died down to a tolerable level and Robert checked his work.

"Nothing. Not even a damn splinter!" He did not expect a large cut but hoped there would be something more than a small indentation where the knife blade cut into the edge of the wood.

Frustration from the outcome and the desperation of their situation became a dangerous combination in Robert's mind, causing logical thought to give way to raw emotion. He picked up the knife, now with a completely different purpose and began stabbing at the floor over and over as hard as he could. Mostly out of anger, but there was a method to this madness. If he could splinter the surface, he may be able to use his knife to drill through the floor. It would be a small hole, but it would be a start. Wildly stabbing, hitting random points inside the same foot-wide circle did nothing. The wood appeared to be wet and each strike of the blade point did nothing more than make an indentation before bouncing off. The ferocity of each strike increased with each bounce as he saw no progress. He was swinging out of fury.

He hated the wood.

He hated the box.

Only a metallurgical breakdown interrupted his efforts when the blade snapped in half at its mid-point.

The metallic ping of the blade breaking made everyone jump and then sigh in depression. Robert didn't think this would work, but he couldn't think of any other options. They were officially trapped now. Without a signal on either cellphone, they couldn't call for help. They had no way to help themselves escape. Robert sat down and leaned back and staring at the opposite wall. His mind was miles away from this place at the moment; trying to escape on its own.

The rest of them followed suit and either lean against the wall or sit.

"Michelle, what time does your phone say?"

Michelle checked the display on her phone. "It is 5:03, Mary. My God, I think we've been in here for three hours."

"Three hours? I was supposed to pick up my kids from the sitter's an hour ago!"

"Mary, do they know where you were going? Does anyone know where any of you were going today?" Robert thought Doug may be on to something with his line of questioning. Amy was at work, so he didn't tell her where he was going, but one of the others probably told someone and they would eventually start looking for them.

Jill responded, "I did. My husband knows I was coming to see a friend, but he doesn't know the address."

There was hope in Doug's voice, "Jill that's great! How long before you think he'll start looking for you?"

"I am not sure. If I wasn't home before he went to work tonight, I'm not sure if he would know I was missing until the morning."

"He wouldn't try to call you or expect you to call him when you got home?"

"No, he's not allowed to have his phone while on the floor."

Dejected by Jill's answer, Doug asked the others. "Dammit! Anyone else?"

Most of the others lived alone or told no one where they were going. Robert remembered Michelle had children. "Michelle, who has your kids?"

"They're with their dad for the weekend, and not due back 'til Monday."

Either no one would realize they are missing or those that would, don't know where they are. Robert zoned out again staring through the wall. There was no way out. They had to wait for what was next.

Silence overtook the group for the next hour with only the occasional rustling of someone moving to get comfortable. Their only source of light flickered off thrusting them back into darkness.

"Sorry, my phone is dead now."

Robert reached into his pocket and pulled his out. "It's okay, I have mine. Looks like we can run it for another thirty minutes or so." He flipped on the light and laid it on the floor.

That light lasted for no longer than thirty minutes and went out about the same time the adrenaline of the situation started to wear off. Robert's mind battled to stay awake, but his body had other ideas and succumbed to the exhaustion. Before he dozed off, his mind got one passing shot in and rolled over and over the details of their current situation. There was no way this was an accident. This box they are in proved this was intentional, but why? His body shut down and he joined the others in their sleep, before his mind could realize there was no answer, yet.

9

Robert's body jerked awake with his mind feeling cloudy and groggy. It took several minutes for him to recognize the dark void and stale air of the small wooden box. Buried in the silence of the box there was a mechanical hum. That must be what Doug heard through the door before. Only now, in the complete silence, Robert heard it. If he focused, he could even feel a slight vibration in the floor. There was another sound or rhythm underneath the hum, but he couldn't make out the source before it stopped and then—there it was again. Maybe an air conditioner cycling or something.

Robert leaned forward to stretch his back. A stiffness radiated from his legs all the way up through his neck as he pushed himself up from the floor. He was half up when a blinding light invaded the box through all the holes and slits. Shielding his eyes from the glare with his right hand, hoping his vision adjusts, Robert stumbled to his feet and leaned against the wall. After a few moments, his eyes adjusted to see the entire box illuminated by light seeping in through every hole in the wall and slit in the floor. Looking up at the ceiling, he saw the negative image of the floor cast by the light coming through the slits.

"Um, guys. You might want to wake up."

Kevin was the first to stir. "What is it..." He stopped his reply in mid-sentence having noticed the light. "Oh, never mind."

Mary asked, "How long has that been on?"

"Just a few minutes before I woke you all. When I woke up, it was still dark and silent, except for the machinery that Doug heard earlier, then suddenly the light came on."

"I want to look outside." Doug bent down to look through a slit in the floor. He pressed his face as flat against the floor as he could; staying there for several seconds until he sat up, rubbing his eye.

"Well Doug, what did you see?"

"The light's too bright. I couldn't see anything."

"Let me try the wall." Robert cupped his hand over one of the holes in the wall and pressed his right eye against his hands. He thought he saw something a foot away but couldn't make out any details. He removed his hands and pressed his eye right up against the hole to see if he can make it out, but no such luck. "I see something just a foot away, but the light is too bright to make out the details."

The rest of them replicated what Robert did, picking different holes and trying to see if any of them could see anything. Jill, Mary, and Kevin all pull back from the wall, rubbing their eyes which watered from the intense light. The only one who continued to try was Doug.

"Guys, this is weird. It looks like a bank of spotlights about ten feet away are pointing at us." Doug picked the first row of holes to look through, but instead of looking at eye-level he got down on the floor and looked out the lowest one. "From this hole I can see the frame and the edge of the bottom light."

The rest of them dropped to the floor to see what Doug saw, but the investigation was short lived. A voice they recognized echoed from above, "Sorry about that. Let's try that again. Hello and welcome, I hope you are doing well."

The occupants of the box exchanged a series of stunned looks. They all recognized the voice, it was Christopher, but now he had a British accent. Without even discussing it, all at once they kicked, banged, and screamed from within the box.

A plea came from outside the box, "Stop. Please Stop." They ignored the plea, if anything the intensity and ferocity of the banging and screaming increased. This resulted in one more demand delivered in an ear-shattering volume and impact, "SILENCE!"

That got everyone's attention. They stopped, startled by the sound and vibrations reverberating through the box and the air itself. Robert heard screaming in the distance for a split second and was not sure if it was an echo or the ringing in his ears. In the silence, bleeding in through the holes, Robert heard the faint sound of music and a recognizable murmur. In complete disbelief he asked himself, "Why would there be a crowd here?"

Robert started to mention the crowd when the speaker kicked in again. "Now that is better. Hello everyone and welcome. I hope you are ready for a day full of fun and games. Each of you have shown you love to play games in the digital world. That is great fun, but also limiting. There is no emotion, no primal stress and fight for survival. Your pulse does not quicken uncontrollably. No cold sweat forming on the back of your neck as you fear what is about to come around the corner. Nothing hangs in the balance other than maybe a little pride. Today all of that will change. You will become involved with the games. You will feel the panic and stress as you ponder how every move you make impacts your chance of survival. You will become the players in the game. There is no respawning and no reset button. All game outcomes are... well, final."

"Oh, and it isn't just for your enjoyment. Oh no, there is no fun in that! This is for all our enjoyment. What do you think; should we bring out our teams?"

Cheering? Robert heard screams and applause, so there was a crowd out there. What is this place and what are they in the middle of? The occupants of the box looked around at each other stunned at the sound of the cheering. They all thought they were there alone at Christopher's house, but now find themselves in the middle of something that sounded like a large sporting event waiting for the teams to enter.

There was a low musical beat in the background that started as soon as Christopher stopped talking, the drum beat audible over the cheering of the crowd. The light that shone through the perforations in their enclosure disappeared, throwing them back in to darkness. Metal-on-metal grinding appeared outside their box. The sound stopped, and the front wall fell forward opening the box for the first time since Kevin closed the door hours ago. A series of spotlights focused on the front opening of the box. Instinctually they all used their hands to shield their eyes.

The voice, the one they used to know as Christopher, started up again on the loudspeaker using a condescending tone, "Come on out, don't be shy."

Not a soul moved. They stayed standing right where they were in the box, shielding their eyes from the spotlights. The thought of walking out of the box they are familiar with and out into a world they could not even see, was not at all attractive. Robert heard the crowd getting restless and starting to "boo" a little.

Kevin yelled from the back, "What the hell is that? Is there a crowd out there?"

Robert responded, "I think so. I thought I heard them earlier, but it sounds like it now." Robert strained his eyes looking into the spot light, trying to look to either side to see if he can see the crowd, but the bright light blocked out everything and caused his eyes to water.

Their vision adjusted, but only if they looked down, Doug slid his foot forward, past the door, looking for footing to make sure he was not about to take a step off a cliff into an abyss. He felts a floor in front of him and took a step forward. He repeated this slide-step combination for the first few steps until he could see the floor clearer.

When Doug was the only outside the box, some verbal "encouragement" was offered to entice the others, "That is it, come on out. You guys come on out too, there is nothing to be afraid of, yet."

Doug, Michelle, and Robert moved forward, but no one else did. Robert could see some features outside now. The lights were suspended from the ceiling on either side of the elevated platform. They were about twenty feet away and pointed straight at them blocking their view of anything beyond the lights. Where either Christopher or the crowd were seated was a mystery.

The platform was a five-foot-wide wooden floor suspended from the ceiling. It extended forward for as far as they could see. Black metal bars surrounded the entire platform, much like the ones you would find in a prison cell. You can tell the platform was hanging from the ceiling, like the lights, as each little movement produced a slight vibration in the platform; not enough to make you feel unsteady, but enough to detect.

Christopher's echoing voice played to the crowd, "I think they need a little encouragement, don't you?"

With the loud cheer from the crowd, Robert felt a vibration traveling through the platform. The vibration was not the crowd, it was too regular and mechanical for that. The vibration grew, the source was below them. Soon the sound of multiple machines starting up drowned out the cheering. They grew louder and were followed by several screams in various voices. The sounds of the machine stopped, but the painful screams and uncontrollable wailing continued. Robert looked around; it wasn't them.

They all looked back and forth at each other with the same questions. Who was screaming and why? Before anyone could say anything to one another, the question of why was answered when the machines started up again, sending the vibration up through the floor of the platform; but now stronger than before. Then the unmistakable high-pitched screaming sound of not one but many circular saws kicked in as the front of edge of twelve-inch spinning saw blades pierce through the slits in the floor. There is a quick scream from the inside their box, followed by a mass of humanity running out of the box and pushing Robert, Michelle, and Doug down on the platform. Doug hits his head on one of the bars and Robert felt his shoulder ram into one at an uncomfortable angle. In severe pain, Robert fought to roll over and get up. He did so in just enough time to see the saw blades disappear beneath the floor. They were followed by one hundred eighteen-inch spinning sharp drill bits plunged into the box through the holes in the walls. There were no screams this time, they were too stunned to scream as they laid there in a mass of humanity wedged between the walls of iron bars. No one was physically injured beyond a few bumps and bruises in the rush to escape the box of horrors.

"Oh good, everyone is out now." A smattering of applause emerged from the darkness. "Shall we start our first game?" The applause exploded into a thunderous level of cheering and stomping that stormed in from the darkness and echoed in the rafters above them. The familiar voice masterfully played to the crowd until he received the response he wanted, "Oh come on. Are you ready?" The intensity of the cheering rose to a level where all the sounds merge into a single thunderous roar that consumed every object it came in contact with. After a few moments it died down, but not until Christopher finished milking it.

"I am sure you will recognize our first competition for the night. It was a childhood favorite of mine, I am sure it was one of yours. Let's show our teams what their first task is." The spotlights focused on the occupants of the box now danced around the ceiling and platform until finally landing on, and illuminating, a large structure hanging below them. The crowd went wild, like their favorite team had entered the stadium.

Michelle leaned close to Robert and asked, "Is that what I think it is?"

Robert did not recognize it when the spotlights first illuminated it but, when Michelle asked, it came into focus. It was absurd to believe what it was, but there was no other explanation.

In front of them, plexiglass panels created walls around the platform. The platform itself had three large holes cut in it. Ladders protruded through the holes leading down to two square structures made of steel I-beams. The structure frames out a grid of three rows and three columns. The squares made by the boxes are large enough for a person to stand in. The ladders were lined up with each of the three columns with plexiglass bridges linking the ladders to the back of the boxes on each row. Plexiglass panels sealed the front of the box. OSB planks bridged the gaps between the squares, creating the floors and walls for each of the boxes.

There was no mistaking it. It was the largest Tic-Tac-Toe board Robert had ever seen.

What had gone unnoticed, until Doug tapped Robert on the arm and pointed, was the second structure facing them with its own platform above it.

"There it is. What do you think everyone?" The crowd showed their approval with a modest round of applause. "Now the rules for our game. We follow the normal rules for Tic-Tac-Toe. We have two teams. Each team will alternate in taking turns. As you can tell though, unlike normal Tic-Tac-Toe, we are not using just one board. Oh no. We are using two boards; one for each team. When a team takes their turn, a player will climb down the ladder for their board and enter a square. Once sealed up in that square the corresponding square on the opposing teams board will close. Three in a row in any direction wins. If there is a tie, we start over and keep playing until we have a winner. Now that we have reviewed our rules, shall we invite our teams to approach their boards? Of course, come closer guys. We would hate for you to drop out before we all have fun."

Robert whispered to himself, "there is another team", then heard simultaneous crashes; one behind him and one in front of him. There was a quick rush from behind him. It pushed him, Michelle, and Doug forward. Robert looked back and saw the platform section that connected to the box had fallen away. They inched forward until they were all completely in the plexiglass enclosed section of the platform— and not a minute too soon—as another series of crashes, again behind him and off in the distance in front of him, sent the last remaining pieces of platform into the dark abyss below. Kevin took one final look behind where the platform used to hang from and then moved as far away from the edge as possible, crowding the others.

A sheet of plexiglass emerged up from the darkness below and pressed up against the platform and the walls creating a clear box around them. Only Kevin took notice of the new enclosure. The others saw the ghostly faces that appeared out of the darkness on the platform above the other game board.

They looked like they have been through a war. Each of them bloodied. Two members appeared to suffer severe injuries. One woman was kneeling, dripping blood while others try to apply pressure to several wounds in her shoulder and upper chest. The wound in her shoulder looks as if it went all the way to the bone. Pieces of flesh and muscle hung from it as if something ripped it off. Robert's thoughts instantly went to the drills and the screams they heard in the distance earlier; she must have still been in the box when they plunged through the holes. The last was a white male in a business suit lying on the platform with blood pooled around him and running down the first ladder. Several members tended to his right leg which was severed just above the ankle. Robert couldn't get over his appearance. His complexion was grey and empty. If he had to capture the picture of death, this is what it would be. He did not flail around or move. Instead he sat calmly, holding his severed foot in his right hand, while his team members worked to stop the bleeding and save his life. These images hammered home the severity of their condition, and for the first time Robert realized they are in a fight of life and death as a cold, sweaty panic overtook his soul.

"All right, there they are. Let's get this started." Christopher let out an exaggerated laugh before continuing. "Okay, all bets in. No more bets." The crowd responded with a groan. Doug looked back at the group and while Robert could not hear his voice, he could see he mouthed, "They are taking bets on us?"

"Before the game I made a random selection of who would go first and let's see... Doug that would be you guys. Your move first."

Robert watched as Doug stood there and searched for the source of the voice. Unable to find it he stood up straight and announced as loud as he could, "We will not play, Christopher! Let us go."

The voice provided a rebuttal, "Oh, yes you will." There was a loud click above them followed by the sound of a large object slowly swinging from side to side. They looked up, but couldn't see anything in the darkness. Each felt the ever so slight feel of a breeze from the swinging object blowing down on their face.

"That sound is your encouragement. Above each of the teams is a twenty-foot-long, sharp, swinging steel blade with a three-hundred-pound pendulum counterweight to keep it moving. That blade is sharp and heavy enough to cut clear through a fifteen-foot-wide hardwood tree. With every swing it lowers down a few inches. In about a minute, it will be down to inches above your heads. Another minute later it will be at about waist level and at the end of three minutes it will be on the platform. So, you do have a choice, but I wouldn't think about it for too long. Your move Doug. Oh, and your team has to go in the order you are standing now."

Doug stood there while the rest of his team felt the stress from the threat above. They screamed at him to move.

Mary yelled the loudest, "Doug, just go. If we play, we survive. Move! Now!"

Michelle gave him a quick shove from behind that sent him stumbling forward toward the ladders. He looked back at the group after regaining his balance. Breaking his protest, Doug picked the center ladder and climbed down to the center row. He stepped on the plexiglass bridge that connected the ladder with the center square and walked across into the square.

Christopher's play-by-play commentary began, "The center square, a classic start."

As soon as Doug's feet hit the OSB floor of the center square, the clear walkway behind him hinged up and sealed him inside the square. The walkway on the corresponding square in the opposing team's game board closed, blocking anyone from entering that square.

The first member of the opposing team, a middle aged, bald white male wearing denim shorts and a red t-shirt, wasted no time at all and hurried across the platform to the first ladder. He descended to the bottom square.

Before his square sealed him in, Michelle was on the move toward the last ladder. She went down the last ladder just one square to enter the top right corner square.

The next to go for the other team was a petite mid-thirties Latino woman dressed for a night in the club, not a day climbing around on ladders. The blood of her teammates was splatted cross her sequined black dress. She was visibly shaken and upset and moved timidly toward the ladders. Robert saw her teammates yelling at her, but he could hear them. She made it to the last ladder on their grid and climbed down to the bottom square, blocking a potential win and end of the game for Robert's team.

It was Robert's turn now, and he wasted no time, motivated by the growing sound of the swinging object approaching them from above, he sprinted to the second ladder and climbed down as fast as he could to the bottom square; leaving the clear bridge with the thought of his team and the blade dominating his mind. He stepped into his square and heard the glass close behind him. He bent down to look up past the frame of his square to see his team. This vantage gave him a glimpse of them, now somewhat crouching down at the intimidating sound of the approaching blade. Even safely in his square he felt the stress of the others as if he were still up on the platform.

The other team was taking too long again. He banged on the glass and screamed, "Come On!" toward the other team, even though he knew no one could hear him. They had the same impending encounter approaching overhead, but this one person seemed to think they had all the time in the world to contemplate their next move. Robert saw her team going nuts. They screamed and gestured for her to move. All while they ducked down to avoid the object that inched closer above them. The stress of the situation appeared to have her confused at what to do as she shuffled a few steps and then paused, shuffled a few more and stopped.

Robert body tensed up watching her move slowly to the ladder of her choice. He felt like a bottled-up bomb ready to explode, but instead of exploding, the pressure released when she picked a ladder. The release was not entirely because she picked a ladder, but the one we picked. She made a mistake. He looked up at his team, now crouched below the blade that swung in and out of his view, and saw hope. Robert looked at the other team and saw disbelief. Each knelt down on the platform, some covered their eyes, and a few cried.

Mary crawled like Spiderman across the platform to the middle ladder. Scurrying down the ladder and into the top center square, completing a column of three players for their team. They won. Across from Robert, the members of the other team were trapped in their squares looking back at him with emotionless expressions. In the squares they could not see where their own members are, but they had a ring-side seat to watch Mary win the game for them. The woman who made the fatal mistake sat on the floor of her square, holding her head in her hands crying and screaming, but she was the only one that will hear her pain.

A click behind Robert freed him and allowed the sounds of the cheering crowd to invade the once quiet square.

Thier master of ceremonies announced, "Well, we have a winner. Well played. Well played. Remember to claim a winning ticket you need both the winning team and the number of moves and it was, seven. Seven total moves. Congratulations and well done. Come on down the ladders to the ground. Come on."

Robert walked out of his square to the ladder and looked up. The swinging blade had disappeared, and the remaining members of his team were descending the ladders. He descended as well. Doug and Michelle were there to meet him; Mary soon joined them. There were no congratulatory high-fives, just a small shared feeling of relief as they were safe on the ground, still wrapped in darkness; but there was no immediate danger in sight.

Looking back up at the opposing team's grid, the squares were still closed, trapping members inside. The ladders had been removed leaving no escape for those up on the platform. They were waiting, waiting for a way down that will never arrive. Those trapped in the squares banged on the glass and created a rumble like a big bass drum.

Doug tapped Robert on the shoulder and pointed out an illuminated door in front of them. The others noticed Robert and Doug looking and turned to see it as well. Robert was not sure if that door was for them to go through or if someone would come out, so he waited. Jill and Mary didn't wait, they took off in that direction.

A few moments later, Christopher provided the confirmation Robert was waiting on, "Congratulations again for a game well played. Please proceed to the door. It is now time for us to say goodbye to the losing team. It was a good attempt, but not good enough. Thank you for your sacrifice."

They walked out as a team, a victorious team, toward a door framed in the bright white rope lights. With only ten feet left to reach the door, a flash of towering flames exploded up through vents in the floor under the opponent's grid and shattered the darkness in the room. In a matter of seconds, the wall of flames roared upwards through the grid and engulfed the platform above it. The plexiglass walls from the grid and the platform focused the flames into a blow torch-like heat. The view of the individuals on the platform was lost in the wall of flames. Each square became its own encapsulated death chamber. They saw the occasional thrashing around of a charred appendage as it involuntarily slammed into the plexiglass. The plexiglass held the sound in, not that you would hear them screaming over the roar of the fire and the cheering of the crowd. A large ball of fire fell from the platform, interrupting the vertical eruption of flame for a few seconds until it hit the floor in an explosion of flame. Robert assumed that was someone falling through one of the openings in the floor where the ladders once stood.

Robert was frozen by the sight of horror happening in front of his eyes. The intense heat seared the side of his face while the images in front of him were scorched into his soul. The thought of watching someone die in front of him causes a visceral response deep inside. His thought about what those in the grid were going through as the flames burned the flesh away from their bones; it was a pain he could not fathom. Just the thought and caused him to feel physically ill. As much as they wanted to turn away and not watch, he and the rest of his team found themselves in a trance watching the horrific deaths of six people they will never know. The inferno hammered home that perilous nature of their situation; that could have been them. Finally he forced himself to break the stare at the macabre exhibit and he walked through the illuminated door trying to leave it behind him but the fear of what is left to come haunted him. Are they done and free to escape now, or does another challenge await them? Robert felt it in his soul, this is not over by a long shot.

10

Hurrying through the illuminated door, they escaped the heat and light from the scene from hell, each witnessed something they would never forget. It changed each of them from that moment forward. Inside the doorway they stood in a circle facing in, looking at one another, but no one said anything. They didn't have to, the looks on their faces and body language said everything. Kevin was bent over with his hands braced on his knees. He alternated between looking at the floor and looking at the others. Jill leaned back against the wall, physically shaken. Doug stood still, looking into the darkness in front of them. Mary sat on the ground with her head in her hands. Bob and Michelle were close to the center of the room looking back at the others, the door was in their line of sight, but they did everything they could to not look at it.

Robert was on his knees, lost in thought, trying to absorb everything going on. He wondered if any of them would survive, would he ever see Amy again, or his family? Was this how someone felt when they face the executioner, emotionally bouncing back and forth between the complete despair of resigning oneself to dying to the ultimate rebellion of looking for any opportunity to survive. He focused on his breathing to calm his thoughts, taking in the brisk coolness this dark room presented. It was peaceful and quiet. He wanted to clear his mind to help him focus, but he can't move the questions or the horror of the last few minutes out of his consciousness.

Exacerbated, Doug asked, "What the hell is happening to us?"

Michelle was the only one to respond as she turned around to survey the room they were in, "I don't know. I don't *fucking* know." She moved farther from the rest of the group to look around the room when several spotlights invaded the cold and quiet tranquility they were recovering in. One light shone on them while the other pointed out a door at the end of the room.

The crowd cheered the appearance of the door and Christopher announced, "Welcome fans to round two." Music played under the cheer of approval and welcomed the arrival of the second round.

As the deafening roar dissolved into an echo in the rafters, the English accented master of ceremonies continued, "That was a great round and well played everyone. well played! Now it is time for our next game. It is one of your favorites making its return. You know it, you love it, I call it Sinking Feeling!" A chorus of "Ooos," and

"Ahs", replaced the normal cheering that followed his announcements. "Yep. Yep. You all know what it is. Let's not waste any time. If our players will now proceed through the door."

Robert absorbed the words Christopher just said. The way he said it hit him a certain way, but before he could make sense of it, he felt a pain run from his feet and up his legs. It stopped to only hit him again a few seconds later, but this time stronger. The sensation caused his knees to give in response, but he felt the muscles in his thighs and calves tighten uncontrollably.

"Come on. Don't make me turn up the electricity!"

No one moved until Jill jumped, letting out a shriek.

"Oh, come now. Don't make me turn up the electrified plate you are all standing on. That was only the first few clicks on the dial I have in my hand; it has twenty clicks. Shall I jump to ten? What do you think everyone?" The crowd starts chanting, "Yes! Yes! Yes!"

Robert remembered this guy just burned people alive, nothing stopped him from inflicting intense pain on them for the enjoyment of others. Whether it was logic kicking in or a survival move, Robert headed for the door. "Come on everyone. I don't want to wait to see what level ten feels like." The crowd approved of their action and cheered again.

In a few seconds they arrived at a turnstile door. Robert went through first and exited into another semi-dark smaller room. He looked around while waiting for the others to join him. One detail stuck out. The door he went through was in the middle of a wall. When he came out, it was in the corner of the room with a wall to its right. The door continued to spin, but no one else emerged yet. He started to worry if he was going to be alone in there, but Kevin came through followed by Michelle and Jill.

Several rows of blue lights turned on overhead revealing what looked like a pool taking up most of the room. The pool walls consisted of multiple squares of metal with a single metal cross piece all joined together. The center of each frame was plexiglass, allowing them to see straight through to the other side. Which gave them a view of a structure in the pool itself, but they could not see it clearly. The spotlights danced around the structure to the crowds delight.

From an overhead speaker, "We have our teams. Now we need our rules." The voice paused while they projected a grid four squares high and four squares wide up on the wall to their right. "Each of you will climb up on the pool deck and then make your way across the bridges to one of the floating squares. The grids on the wall represent the grids you will find in your pools, but the grid you see is not *your* grid, it is the grid for the other team's pool. We identify each square in the grid by two numbers: the column number followed by the row number. For example, if you want to pick the third square from the top in the first row, you will call out three-one. Do you see how this works?"

Christopher waited for a response, but none arrived. "The teams will take turns, calling out one square at a time where they believe someone on the opposing team stands. If someone from the opposing team is standing in that square, they are eliminated from the game. The first team to eliminate all the opponents wins. Those are the rules of the game. Now shall we get this game started? All bets in. No more betting."

The floor below the four of them jerked and started rising. It continued moving silently until it was even with the pool deck where that edge appeared to lock in. The edge of the floor furthest from the pool kept moving up, higher and higher, creating an increasingly sharp tilt toward the pool. Trying to stay upright on your feet became an exercise in futility as the floor approached an insane angle that made Robert feel like he was looking straight down at the pool. Standing with his right leg extended and leaning into the incline with his bent left leg he felt both feet slide. He reached down with his left hand for anything to grab hold of, but the floor was completely smooth and slick.

The floor finally reached an angle that caused gravity to overcome friction, sending everyone sliding down the floor and across a clear surface that covered the pool. The surface was individual squares of plexiglass with rows of holes drilled in them. Each team member came to rest on a single square. A second or so later the unused squares dropped to the bottom, sending mini-explosions of water towering through each now-open square.

The structure they saw earlier in the pool became clearer now. The entire grid was plexiglass boxes that extended from the water line to the bottom of the pool. Metal strips that also served as elevator risers to raise and lower the top piece reinforced the corners.

The four of them made it to their feet, standing up on their squares. Jill asked what no one else in the room had realized yet: There were seven of them when they started through the door, "Where is everyone else?"

Robert hadn't taken the time to wonder about this yet, but it only took him a second to reach the only answer there was: "Jill, I think they're the other team."

"But wait, there are only three of them and there are four of us."

Kevin pointed out, "That could be considered both an advantage and a disadvantage. We have a larger team, so there are more people for them to eliminate, but we also have more targets for them to hit; not as many empty spots."

The voice from overhead started the game, "Now that everyone is in place. Let's begin. Doug, your team goes first again."

After a period of complete silence a small explosion of water erupted from the square in front of Robert. They missed.

"Jill, it is now your team's turn."

Jill screamed as loud as she can, "I don't want to pick!"

"Jill, you don't have to. It is our team's pick." Kevin looked at everyone, waiting for someone else to say something. No one did, so he picked. "One–three." A square of pool water replaced the square in the first column, third row in the projected grid.

Both teams missed, and the crowd showered them in "Boo!"

Jill screamed as her square fell to the bottom of the pool. She struggled to orientate herself and swim back up to the top. Her right hand breached the top of the water and searched for the edge of her box. Finally finding it, she pulled herself up, raising her head above the water; hanging on for her life.

Kevin yelled over to her, "Are you okay?"

Jill didn't say anything. Even if she wasn't, there was nothing they could do. Several cubes of water separated them from her.

Michelle turned back to the grid, pissed off, and called out, "Three–four!"

The bottom square in the third column was replaced by the image of Doug falling into the water.

"That's one there, two left. Let's end this thing." Michelle had a look of determination Robert had never seen. "I want to see my kids again. I'm not going to die." She turned to face the back of the room where we assume the crowd was and screamed, "DO YOU HEAR ME? I AM *NOT* GOING TO DIE IN HERE!"

During her protest the water in the square to Kevin's right splashed. Another miss.

Robert made eye contact with Michelle and announced, "Two–two."

The second square in the second column on the grid flickered to show Mary falling into the water. Michelle pumped her fist at the sight of it. Robert recognized this was where everything changed: yes, they were their friends, but they were also in the way of their own survival. He wanted to see Amy again; Michelle wanted to see her kids again; Jill and Kevin wanted to get out of here alive to rejoin their lives as well. It was us or them, and they must do everything possible to make sure it was not them. He found his feelings about this rather surprising, having never been faced with a life or death decision before. He did not expect to be able to throw away the consideration of a friend's life over his own without any ill-feelings of guilt.

While Robert pondered on this, Kevin made another pick that missed. The other team missed too, picking the square three squares away from Michelle.

"Michelle, you pick next. There is only one of them left. Look up at the board and end this." She studied the board and selected, "Three–one."

All four sets of eyes focused on the wall, waiting for the response. The first square in the third column flickers and showed an empty square of water. Robert dropped his head a little. They missed. The shower of boos and cheers of "You suck!" came from the crowd.

The plexiglass floor below Kevin dropped and dumped him into the cube of water below him. Robert watched as Kevin hit the bottom of the cube and then kicked back to the top of his cube. He grabbed the top edge and pulled himself up above the surface of the water. As soon as his head cleared the water, he yelled above the cheering crowd, "I am okay. End this!"

Robert announced, "Four -two." He did not look at the grid, He just listened for the crowd's reaction. The cheers told him what he needed to here, Bob fell into the water, ending the game.

The squares below Jill and Bob moved up from the bottom of the pool, slowly reaching their feet and continued to lift them back to the top of their cube. Kevin stood strong on his square, but Jill collapsed in a pool of flesh on hers. The remaining squares returned to the top of the pool as well, creating a solid floor across the pool. The grid on the wall changed to show the entire pool containing their friends, now all in the water in the plexiglass cubes that make up the grid.

The speaker overhead crackled to life, "Bravo! Bravo! Congratulations on another well-played game."

Robert remembered a time when he used to enjoy talking to Christopher, now he wished he would just shut up. His wish didn't come true.

"Now I thought it would take longer, what about you? Did you guess the correct team and number of moves? Let me see." He sounded more like the ring master of a circus as he played to the crowd. "Someone did. You know what that means. Ticket one-three-eight-seven needs to step forward." The cheering stopped, but a murmur circulated throughout the crowd as they searched for the lucky ticket holder. Moments later they were located.

"Well congratulations. What is your name?" The entire crowd laughed. "Sorry about that, we don't use names here. So, for picking the right team and number of moves you get to press the button to dispose of the losing team."

A panicked look came over Robert, Jill, and Kevin. Robert knew what happened in the last game. It was horrible enough to watch when it happened to people he didn't know and had never met, but these were his *friends*. As much as he pushed away the thought of them behind his need to survive earlier, he still couldn't handle the thought of something happening to them and he absolutely *couldn't* watch.

Michelle put her head down and walked toward a door on the opposite wall. She didn't look at the image projected.

The crowd chanted, "Now! Now! Now!"

Robert and Jill followed Michelle. They focused on the door and tuned out the crowd and the image on the wall. Kevin stayed fixated on the image of their friends.

The chant changed to a cheer; Robert could only assume the lucky winner pressed the button. He didn't want to think about what happened. The three of them reached the door, but Kevin hadn't moved. He stood where he did for the game, locked on the image projected on the wall. Robert saw tears rolling down his cheeks. "Kevin, come on now. Let's get through this together."

Kevin took a few sideways steps toward the door, stumbling while he kept his focus on the screen. He stumbled again but recovered, this time he turned and ran to the door. He did not stop until he was inside the next room.

Once all four were through the door, the lights turned off behind them and the door closed. This was the smallest room they have been in so far. Kevin headed to the corner furthest away from anyone and sat down. His head buried in his hands as he cried with an occasional violent outburst and slam of his fist into the wall.

Michelle asked, "Kevin what happened?"

Kevin didn't even acknowledge her.

She pressed him further, "Kevin, what happened to them?"

"You don't want to know. None of you want to know."

"I do. That is why I asked."

Kevin jumped to his feet and ran over to Michelle. He stopped inches from her and screamed, "You want to know what happened, Michelle! You want to know what happened to our friends? The cubes they were in turned over, trapping them below the water and they drowned. They all drowned! They are dead, just like we will all be. It is just a matter of time and how. This is a big game to 'Christopher' or whoever he is. It's a game. We are all dead, nothing we can do will change that."

Michelle stumbled backwards until she hit the wall. Sliding down the wall to the floor, she sat expressionless, unable to process what she just heard, but had already realized. It was a common feeling in the room. Each of them held on to a hope that they would find a way out of this; a way to survive. What Kevin said was the unavoidable truth. They are all going to die, it was only a question of when and how.

11

No one had spoken since Kevin told them what had happened to the others. They hadn't looked at each other either. Robert was lost in thought, thoughts that ran continuously in his head. He was in a room with three others, but he might as well be the only person on the planet as he felt a level of loneliness and despondency that isolated and trapped him in his own mind; ignoring the surroundings. Locked within himself, his thoughts moved like a movie from scene to scene documenting all the moments in life he will never be able to experience and the people he will never see again. He saw Amy's face, then how their first-born child would look, and then a Christmas morning all together with his family. He hadn't cried; he hadn't done anything. Just stood there in thought; mentally, physically, and emotionally exhausted. He was not the only one. The other three were as well. Lost in those thoughts almost forgetting where they were, not worried about what was next but more resigned to what fate had dealt them.

A quick but violent jerk shook the room send Michelle running to the center of the room to join the others. All four stood huddled in the dead-center of the room looking out for the source of the shaking. A light emerged from the corners of the room and where the walls meet both the floor and ceiling. The light got brighter and exposed gaps along the edge of the wall that constantly increased in size, slowly opening the small room up into another larger room. The ceiling lifted away and exposing the lights hanging from the rafters of the warehouse. The walls retreated into the vastness that was the larger room. The refuge and seclusion they provided was gone and, they were once again exposed and on display.

The familiar murmur of the crowd and arrival of the spotlight did not surprise them, instead it announced the start of the next challenge in the fight to stay alive. Still numb, there was no sense of adrenaline ran through them. No sense of confusion or terror either. Their fate had been accepted. Robert heard the pop and hum of a speaker above him and took a deep breath, his mind was empty now. Nothing mattered; the end was already settled.

"Wow. Wow is all I can say. This is great, isn't it everyone?" The master of ceremonies worked the crowd and they respond to every prompt. "This has been an exciting night, but the best is yet to come. We have *one* more game, just one more contest to find our winners. Are you ready?"

Right on cue, the crowd roared to life in a ferocity that caused the ground itself to rumble under their feet. The vibration in the floor pulled Robert from the self-imposed solitary confinement. "Kevin, the floor is hollow. Can you feel it moving?"

Kevin looked at Robert and then at the floor, then back at Robert. Kevin raised his leg up almost waist high and then sent it crashing down into the floor with all his might. It created a deep thunderous boom that sent waves through the floor. A slight glimmer of hope crept in. If this floor was some sort of platform, then there was a space underneath and there may be a way out. They needed to break through. He yelled to the others and pointed down, "The floor is hollow, we need to break through!"

Jill looked at Robert like he had gone insane. "Why?"

"There may be a way out in the space below us. Everyone jump. Let's see if we can break through." Not waiting for anyone else, Robert started to jump up and down. Each jump produced a muffled and explosive boom accompanied by a noticeable rise and drop of the floor. After the first few jumps, Kevin joined in. Their efforts did not go unnoticed.

"Oh, I wouldn't do that. In this room, the only way to go is up. Down is not where you want to go, now is it?" The ever-obedient audience responded to the puppet master's strings with a combined chuckle. "Shall we show them what awaits them?" A cargo net unfurled from the roof with the bottom end landing in front of them. Strapped to the bottom edge are two other ropes, with what looked like belts connected to either end. "There it is. The path to victory. All you must do is climb up to the top. Reach the top first then you win your freedom. Come in second? Well, you don't win."

Spotlights moved up and down the net. Robert tried to guess how tall the climb was. He thought back to his days of playing high school football and the distances on a football field. He saw two ten-yard segments making it twenty yards, about sixty feet tall. He could climb that easily. The only question in his mind was does he trust what Christopher said. The person who made it to the top would win and be free. The little bit of hope he felt when he thought they might be able to escape through the floor was cautiously growing.

He sized-up the competition. He was younger than the others, and obviously in better shape. Jill and Kevin should be tired after struggling in the pool. He thought he could easily beat Michelle up the net. He stepped forward and grabbed the net.

"Not yet. Not that way. First, we need to set the teams. All events are a *team* event."

How do you make climbing up a net a team event? Robert was about to ask, when Christopher continued.

"You guys know how much I enjoy teams and remember we always let the game determine the teams in random. So here we go. I will toss a coin. Heads: Jill and you are teamed with Robert, tails: you are teamed with Michelle. It is…" there was a pause for dramatic effect that seemed to last forever. They each want to climb and get this over with.

"HEADS! Jill, you are teamed with Robert. Michelle, you are teamed with Kevin. If you look at the net in front of you, you will see something attached to the net. Those two ropes attached to the net have belts on either end. Each team is to pick and remove one of the ropes from the net and strap in. Once both are strapped in, you will start climbing the net as a team. If one person moves slower, then the entire team will be slowed down. As the saying goes: 'a team is only as strong as its weakest link'." Christopher laughed again, and Robert thought about the opportunity to see him again and give him something to laugh about. "To win, both of you must be at the top before the other team. One member of the team reaching the top first does not count. The entire team must reach the top before the other team to win. Now if the four of you will go ahead and pair up and strap in, we can start."

Michelle stepped forward and unfastened one rope from the net. She handed the other end to Kevin and then strapped herself in. Kevin followed her lead and strapped in. Robert retrieved the remaining rope. Jill was frozen where she stood. Robert walked over to her with the rope and tried to hand her a belt, but Jill did not take it. Robert looked at the glazed look in her eyes and said, "Jill, come on take it. We can get to the top and get out of here, but I can't do it without your help. Let's go." There was no response, only a frozen expression. Robert pleaded to Jill again, "Jill come on! This is our only way. We can take them easily, but I need your help. Take the belt." Nothing.

Christopher noticed Jill's refusal to participate and encouraged her in a rather pouty British accent, "Aww, looks like Jill does not want to play anymore. What a shame. Guess we have to call her and Robert out of this game, right now. What do you all think?" A chorus of boos and jeers filled the open space.

Robert felt desperate and did not want to lose the chance to survive. He considered strapping Jill in himself and dragging her up the net, but was not sure if he would have the strength.

"Jill! Come on. I don't want to die!" Finally, she snapped out of it. She said nothing, just reached and yanked the belt out of Robert's hands and strapped in. Robert strapped in and walked to the net; Jill followed.

Both teams stood at the base of the net. They are participants in a race toed up to the start line. The spotlights raced up and down the net, which appeared to be the star of this sport, not the participants themselves.

"Here we go. We have a great match up here. The winning team is the first one to come up and meet me here at the top. Win and be free. Lose and, well…we all know what will happen, don't we?" Another prompt for the crowd's benefit, and they showed their appreciation with a reaction. "Okay, everyone set? All bets in. Let's get this started!"

The spotlights stopped, and overhead red lights casted eerie, red shadows down through the net for a few seconds then bright white lights flooded the entire room from above simultaneously with the order: "GO!"

Ignoring the watering of his eyes caused by the instantaneous flash of the bright white lights violating his irises, Robert reached up as high as he can on the cargo net and climbed. First hands and then feet. He reached up again and grabbed next rung and then stepped up again. He continued this for four rungs on the net before the rope attached to him went taut. Jill was just taking her first steps on the net. The rope made sure he had to wait for her. To his right, he saw both Michelle and Kevin on the net below him, but above Jill. The rope slackened-up and he moved up another rung.

Focused on the net, he felt a slight movement in the net followed by a cheer in the crowd. He looked down toward Jill, hoping to see a good bit of progress. Instead of noticing that she had only progressed one rung since the last time he looked, he noticed the floor beneath her has fallen away and the net hangs over a dark open void with water running down the sides into nothingness. Before this, Robert felt secure on the net at this height, but the fear of falling now crept into his mind. What was at the bottom of the hole? Sharp blades? Rocks? Or are there other objects to impart unbearable pain on any soul unlucky enough to fall?

His grip tightened on the rung and the rope connecting him to Jill felt like it weighed one thousand pounds. Deliberately, he loosened the grip with his right hand and reached up to the next rung, being careful to make sure he got a firm grasp before he made another move. With his right hand hanging onto the rope on the next rung, he moved his right foot up and stepped into that hole in the net. He repeated the maneuver with his left and felt the rope connecting him to Jill tighten, reminding him she was moving slower than he was.

To move up one single rung in the net took almost a minute, at this rate it would take almost an hour to reach the top. He checked on Michelle and Kevin to his right, they were still below him, but they are next to one another moving together at the same pace. Jill must speed up for them to win. It won't matter if he reaches the top first; if Kevin and Michelle beat Jill up the net, they lose.

"Come on Jill. We can do this!" Robert became her own personal cheerleader, but she did not respond. Her pace stayed as slow as it was before. He watched her and let her move up a few rungs on the net before he made any moves. He felt the frustration build. His life depended on her. After everything they have seen, he did not want to be on the losing end of this. She should realize the same thing and dig down deep for whatever it took to win, but she appeared frozen and disconnected from the situation. He yelled down at her, "Come on Jill. We need to move. We must beat them. If we don't, we die!"

Jill looked up at him with a blank expression on her face and then back at the net before she took another slow step. The muscles in his body tensed, as a renewed flood of adrenaline and stress built up to the point of wanting to explode. He wanted to climb as fast as he could to release the pent up aggression, but he couldn't because of the dead weight strapped to him at the end of a rope.

Robert's mental attitude didn't need any help to turn to anger at this point, but when Michelle and Kevin pulled even to him on the net, that was the last straw. He gave the rope quick tug and yelled down at Jill, "I am *not* going to die because of you. I'm going to live even if I have to drag your ass up this net!" He gave her another tug. They were only a few feet up at this point, there was such a long way to go. He scaled up two rungs, locked his feet into the net and wrapped his right hand in the net to secure himself. While he yelled at Jill to move, he used every ounce of muscle-strength he had in his body and pulled the rope up causing her to increase her pace. He dropped the rope and raced up again as far as he could go until there he was out of slack.

Once again, he locked himself in place with his feet and right hand and used his left side to yank Jill up. When she stopped, she glared up at him and said, "Stop it. You are going to make me fall!"

Her warning did not deter Robert. One more time he scurried up as far as he could go; locked in and looked down at Jill. She made progress, but not fast enough. He gave the rope a pull to encourage her to pick up the pace again. Robert was ahead in the lead, but Jill was next to the other team. They had to beat them up to the as a team. With a good bit of slack in the rope he made a quick move up, this time covering almost ten feet of the net. They were probably twenty feet up in total and if he had to guess another forty or so to go.

He felt the rope slacken and made his move and then locked in again. Instead of reaching down to pull Jill, he took a moment to recover from the exertion. In these few moments he took in his surroundings. The cheering and screaming crowd was barely audible over the roar of the falling water below him. Spotlights followed their progress up the net. Being almost halfway up the net when he looked down into the dark void below them, he felt a sense of the height and the dizzying sensation of vertigo. Robert gripped the net with both hands to steady his senses and balance. Heights had never bothered him before but dangling above something that resembled a bottomless pit was a little different.

Jill moved at a steady pace now and had gained on Robert. His mind argued with itself. He knew know he needed to move but his instincts of survival wanted to stay firmly attached to the net. It was not until Jill yelled down at him from above that he broke the stalemate and took another step. He was now the lowest of all of them on the net.

Seeing her up there restored his hope and helped him forget about his minor moment of height related panic. He rushed up and pulled even with Jill, about twenty-five feet up. Michelle and Kevin were yelling at each other, they knew they were behind and tried to force each other to pick up the pace. The net started to sway and, at first, Robert thought the increased pace and movement of all four of them in the same area of the net caused it, but as the movement became larger, it formed waves that start at the top and moved down. Christopher had added a new challenge.

The waves slowed the progress of both teams. Everyone was careful to ensure they had a firm grip with one hand or foot before letting go with the other. The movement made it more difficult to grab the ropes that crisscrossed through the net. As you reached for one, the movement moved it out of your grasp.

One hand and one foot at a time, Jill and Robert climbed the net. Fatigue set into both causing their hands and forearms to burn and their legs to shake. Robert assessed where they are. Only ten feet away from the top, but the closer they are, the faster the waves came. Jill had wrapped the net in her arms and hung on with everything she has. They cannot stop now, they were almost to the top.

"Jill, we're almost there. Just a few more steps and we can grab the top edge." Robert's encouragement caused Jill to look up and see it too. She reached up with her right hand and grabbed the next horizontal rope going across the net. When she tried to pull herself up, the peak of a wave hit her and threw her off the net. Robert watched in slow motion as Jill tumbled from above him and off the net. Before he realized what he saw, all of Jill's weight ripped at Robert's lower back and torso through the rope. His feet were pulled from the net, but his heavily fatigued arms and hands hung on. As her momentum yanked to a stop, she swayed back to the net. This allowed Robert to get one foot back on the net. The waves and strain kept him from getting a solid foothold with the other. His forearms burned, and he felt the tearing of the individual strands of muscle and tendons connecting his chest to his shoulder.

Out of the corner of his eye, he helplessly watched Michelle and Kevin move up the net. They were within six feet or so of grabbing the top edge. He was unable to move up, Jill's weight at the end of a ten-foot rope and gravity pulled him backwards and down. Jill fought to turn herself around and grab the net. Her struggle put even more strain on Robert making the entire situation more perilous. She needed to stop, but if she did, she would only dangle at the end of the rope and Robert knew he couldn't drag them both up. He had an idea, an act of desperation brought on by the sight of Kevin and Michelle moving further up the net. He could use one hand to turn Jill around and swing her back to the net, but it was risky to try to support both of their weight with one arm. He took his right hand and forearm and wrapped it around, first a vertical rope and then a horizontal rope. He pulled on it several times to make sure it was secure and then let go with his left hand. Their combined weight was instantly routed through his right shoulder down into his chest. He felt muscles strain and burn and an unbearable pain in his shoulder joint.

Robert reached down with his right hand and tried to twist the rope connecting him to Jill. She turned, but because of the waves rolling down the net, her attempt to grab it missed. She would have to spin all the way around before she could make another attempt. Robert tried to swing her back and forth to get her closer to help her next attempt. To his horror, he felt the nylon threads of the rope dig in and burn his forearm as his grip started to slip. The pain sensations conflicted with his drive to survive, the pain told him to let go, but his survival instinct won't let it happen. Jill turned around toward the net and reached out with her left arm to try to grab it, but it remained out of reach. She needed to turn a little more to be in range, but there may not be time for that. Robert's forearm and grip slipped in the tangle of flesh and nylon; a last-ditch death grip grab with his right hand saved them. With the muscles in the palm of his right hand burning, and a shoulder that feels like it is now out of the joint, he reached up with his left hand to help support the weight, but gravity had a different plan for him though. His right hand gave, and he found himself separated from the net. It was a sensation he was not able to process; his mind didn't know how to react as he saw himself passing Jill as she grabbed the net. Robert's weight and momentum ripped her from the safety of the net. Robert's mind wandered to visions of Amy's smile; thoughts of his family, his favorite song. There was no sensation of falling as he and Jill disappeared into the black abyss of the hole below them. No grand goodbye, no grand realization about the end of his existence. He didn't even hear the reaction from the crowd that has been enthralled by the drama unfolding before them. His mind was lost in his random musings until he loses consciousness.

12

Robert woke up groggy in a dark room on a cot. Through the haze in his head he heard sounds off in the distance, but his eyes were still blurry and couldn't make anything out other than moving shapes in the distance. He laid there trying to understand what was going on. He did not remember anything before he woke up in this room.

He tried to prop himself up on his elbows to look around more, but instantly fell back flat on the cot. As soon as he put any weight on his right elbow, his right shoulder shot a pain message to his brain he could not ignore. Robert reached up with his left hand to feel his right shoulder and noticed a bandaged wrapped around it. He had been injured somehow. He slid his hand down his right arm and found the edge of the bandage in the middle of his bicep. There was another just past his elbow on his forearm. It didn't feel broken, but when he pressed on the bandage a shooting pain and an image of him hanging from a net by one arm appeared in his head. The image disappeared as quickly as the pain, but the memory of the image remained. Rolling it around in his head, he pieced together a few other images and put the jagged puzzle together.

Someone held him against his will. Who? Christopher; he remembered that now. Christopher forced them to play in life or death games, the last one involved climbing up a net and he and someone else fell. He didn't die. He didn't die. Now what? Is he still in danger and... where the hell was he?

The sound of two familiar voices pulled him from his own thoughts and produced a layer of cold sweat on his brow. He could not hear what Michelle or Christopher were saying, but he knew their voices. This left him to assume he was still in danger and needed to get out. Deciding to lay there until the right time, he considered his options, which were rather limited. He didn't know where he was, nor did he know where to run to when the chance presented itself.

He felt someone rub his forehead and jumped.

"Hey there. How're you feeling?"

He opened his eyes to see Michelle leaning over his head looking down at him. Ignoring the pain in his shoulder, he jumped from the cot and landed stumbling and sliding on the glossy white tiled floor. His lack of coordination sent him crashing into a stainless-steel table with bandages and ointments on it.

Michelle moved toward him. "Whoa, Robert! Take it easy. Everything is okay. You're fine." He looked back with fear in his eyes.

"Christopher, Kevin, Doug, someone get in here!"

Robert staggered to his feet and ran out the door. The white tile continues outside the room and into the hallway. With no clue which way to go, Robert ran to the right. He made it about twenty feet until he saw Christopher and Kevin coming with others he did not recognize...or did he?

He turned around and ran in the opposite direction past Michelle as she stood in the doorway of the room. There were other doors in this section of the hallway. Robert tried the first door, but it was locked. He tried the next, it was locked as well. As he ran to the third, he heard a voice from down the hallway, "Hey Robert. Relax." Robert knew that voice. It was Doug, but...Doug was *dead*. His team lost in the pool; Kevin said they drowned.

Doug walked around the corner with his arms outstretched with his palms up, "Robert, calm down. We can explain."

"Doug, I was told you died."

"I know, man. Relax, I know this is all confusing. Just have a seat there and we can explain."

From behind him he heard a new voice, "Robert, sweetie. You're safe. Calm down." The voice was not one that he expected. He spun around and saw Amy walking toward him. A flood of emotions and confusion hit him as he collapsed to the ground right there in the hallway. Amy rushed to him, but Robert passed out again before she reached him.

13

Robert woke up feeling groggy again in the same room he woke up in moments earlier. This time he remembered instantly what had happened and started to get up, but noticed two people sitting next to him on the bed. He opened his eyes and saw Amy. She sat there and held his hand and Christopher sat next to him on the other side. He glanced around the room and saw Jill, Bob, Doug, Mary, Michelle, and Kevin. Taking a quick glance at the doorway he saw others that he recognized as the other team they first met during the Tic-Tac-Toe game. The man in the door was missing a leg then, but here he was, standing fine on two healthy legs.

Amy patted his hand to get his attention back on her. "How are you feeling, baby?"

Robert provided an answer that was the understatement of the year. "Confused. *Very* confused."

A small giggle filled the room.

Christopher, who was not in a wheelchair and still had the British accent that only revealed itself after they were all released from the box, said. "Robert, you are confused just like everyone is their first time."

"First time? Christopher what the hell is this? You trapped us and held us for hours if not days. You made us compete against others and killed people. I watched them die, but..."

"But, no one died Robert. As you can see here, everyone is still very much alive and healthy. I am sorry about your forearm. The rope we use is coated with a covering that is not supposed to rip the skin. As for watching people die. Yes, you watched people die and as of the last count I received, almost twenty-three million others did all around the globe via the dark web."

Robert, more confused than before, grabbed Christopher's arm and interrupted him demanding, "WHAT DO YOU MEAN: WATCHED?"

"My friend, this is a game show. A reality show of sorts that is broadcast on shadow sites all around the world. People pay to watch and bet on the action."

"A FUCKING SHOW! You kidnapped me for A FUCKING SHOW?"

"Kidnapped is such a harsh word. I admit our methodology is one that is questionable, but it is how we have done this for several years now and it produces the best shows."

The anger swelled in Robert. "Questionable methodologies? Enlighten me. What did you do to me?"

Christopher got up and walked, yes walked, to the foot of the cot. "Well... first you are still in the warehouse I live in. You have only been here for three hours. The soda you drank had a few knockout drops in it. I find having you wake up disoriented when the games begin creates a more genuine and believable reaction; Realism is especially important. Everyone has to believe what they are seeing is real. No one dies, no one is supposed to get hurt. It is all special effects, again to make everything seem real. Your friends over there." Christopher pointed to where his friends stood. "They have been part of this with me for the last nine months. I have four groups of folks we rotate to keep anyone watching from realizing someone they thought died on the last show is suddenly alive on another show. You were lucky, someone left our little cast, and we needed to add one more. We always keep the newbies in the dark for the first time, again or the realism. After the..."

"Wait!" Robert interrupted again. He rubbed his forehead with his left hand and sat up. "Let me get this straight. This is all for a web show?" Now looking at everyone in the room. "You ALL, lead me over here under false pretenses. Held me against my will and then forced me to play games that I thought were life or death. All for just a stupid web show?"

Christopher nodded. "Basically, yes." With that blunt answer, a combination of confusion and disbelief consumed Robert's face "It *must* be that way, or it does not seem real and then no one watches. Once you do it and understand then you know how to react to sell it and you will even enjoy it. Look how real your friends sold it, you have gotten to know each of them and their reactions had you convinced this was all real. It is what people want to see."

"No way, uh-uh. That is not going to happen, buddy. I'm not going to do this. No way, no how. I'm going to the cops and shutting this all down. You all, and even the crowd, are going to jail."

"Oh, there is no crowd. Those sounds are added for the *appearance* of a crowd. The only ones involved are those you see in this room and another five people that help with the production side of things." Kevin handed a large envelop to Christopher. "And before you go to the cops, maybe you should count what is in the envelope, that is your take of the show. Should be a quarter of a million."

Christopher dropped the envelope on the cot next to Robert with a thud. Robert made note of the thickness and weight and opened it. He did not know what to say anymore. In his hand he had an envelope with a quarter of a million dollars. He looked up at his girlfriend with hope she would help center him, but her face created another question. "Amy, why are you here? You were at work."

Amy with all the honesty and compassion of an angel, "You thought I was at work, but I was coming here. I've been watching this show online at night for months. How do you think they found you?"

GAME MASTER

Follow the SanSquad in their next adventure in Part 2, Game Master: Playing for Keeps.

WHAT DID YOU THINK OF GAME MASTER: GAME ON?

First of all, thank you for purchasing Game Master: Game On. I know you could have picked any number of books to read, but you picked this book and for that I am extremely grateful.

I hope that it provided you a few moments of enjoyment. If so, it would be really nice if you could share this book with your friends and family by posting to *Facebook* and *Twitter*.

If you enjoyed this book and found some benefit in reading this, I'd like to hear from you and hope that you could take some time to post a review. Your feedback and support will help this author to greatly improve his writing craft for future projects and make this book even better.

You can follow this link to *Game Master: Game On* now.

GET YOUR FREE READERS KIT

Subscribe to David Clark's Reader's Club and in addition to all the news, updates, and special offers available to members, you will receive a free book just for joining.

Get Yours Now! – https://mailchi.mp/8d8c7323151e/davidclarkhorror

ABOUT THE AUTHOR

David Clark is an author of multiple self-published thriller novellas and horror anthologies (amazon genre top 100) and can be found in 3 published horror anthologies. His writing focuses on the thriller and suspense genre with shades toward horror and science fiction. His writing style takes a story based on reality, develops characters the reader can connect with and pull for, and then sends the reader on a roller-coaster journey the best fortune teller could not predict. He feels his job is done if the reader either gasps, makes a verbal reaction out loud, throws the book across the room, or hopefully all three.

You can follow him on social media.
Facebook - https://www.facebook.com/DavidClarkHorror
Twitter - @davidclark6208

ALSO BY DAVID CLARK

Have you read them all?

Standalone Novels

The Ghosts of Miller's Crossing

Death was what sent Edward Meyer away thirty years ago.
Death was what brought him and his children back to Miller's Crossing.

He wanted a quiet and peaceful setting to start over in, but instead he found dark truths, a centuries old family secret, and a war as old as time itself.

The more he uncovered about his past, the more he began to wonder... had he chosen the right side.

If you enjoy paranormal thrillers like "The Shining", "Doctor Sleep", and "The Exorcist", you'll love taking this journey with Edward. Buy THE GHOSTS OF MILLER'S CROSSING today.

Highway 666 Series

Book One – Highway 666

A collection of four tales straight from the depths of hell itself. These four tales will take you on a high-speed chase down Highway 666, rip your heart out, burn you in a hell, and then leave you feeling lonely and cold at the end.

Stories Include:

- Highway 666 - The fate of three teenagers hooked into a demonic ride-share.
- Till Death – A new spin on the wedding vows
- Demon Apocalypse - It is the end of days, but not how the Bible described it.
- Eternal Journey - A young girl is forever condemned to her last walk, her journey will never end

Book Two – The Splurge

A collection of short stories that follows one family through a dysfunctional Holiday Season that makes the Griswold's look like a Norman Rockwell painting.

Stories included:

- Trick or Treat – The annual neighborhood Halloween decorating contest is taken a bit too far and elicits some unwilling volunteers.
- Family Dinner – When your immediate family abandons you on Thanksgiving, what do you do? Well, you dig down deep on the family tree.

- The Splurge – This is a "Purge" parody focused around the First Black Friday Sale.
- Christmas Eve Nightmare – The family finds more than a Yule log in the fireplace on Christmas Eve

Game Master Series

Book One – Game Master – Game On
Robert thought it was just a game. Now he is in a fight to survive.

Robert Deliuz enjoyed passing his time with a group of friends in the world of online video games. A chance meeting changed his perspective and made him the subject of the game. He faces horrifying round after round, struggling to survive while he watches his friends die all around him. At the end, will he stand victorious as Game Master, or will it be GAME OVER?

If you like movies like Saw, Escape Room, and similar stories, then you will love the Game Master series, the latest from international bestselling author David Clark.

Buy book one, Game Master: Game On and see if you have what it takes to be the Game Master.

Book Two – Game Master – Playing for Keeps
Robert thought he understood the game. What he knew was all a lie.

Robert and his wife are enjoying the good life, but not everyone is happy to see that. Their survival let a serious deception out of the bag. One that rubs the true Game Masters the wrong way. Motivated by anger and money, these individuals step out of hiding and devise a plan to be repaid. The price... the blood of those that betrayed them.

If you like movies like Saw, Escape Room, and similar stories, then you will love the Game Master series, the latest from international bestselling author David Clark.

Buy book two, Game Master: Playing for Keeps and to find out the dark truth behind the game.

Book Three – Game Master – Reboot
The Game Masters went too far, now it is time for the players to take the game back.

With one of their own in danger, Robert and Doug reach out to players from the very first group, Alpha, to mount a rescue. During their efforts, Robert finds himself immersed in a Cold War battle to save their friend. Their adversary, an ex-KGB super spy, now turned arms dealer, who is considered one of the most dangerous men walking the planet. Will the skills Robert learned playing the game help him in this real world raid? There are no trick CGIs or trap doors here, the threats are all real.

If you like movies like Saw, Escape Room, and similar stories, then you will love the Game Master series, the latest from international bestselling author David Clark.